# CORY

Corazon Aquino and the Philippines

# CORY

## Corazon Aquino and the Philippines

BEATRICE SIEGEL

LODESTAR BOOKS  E. P. DUTTON  NEW YORK

*Library of Congress Cataloging in Publication Data*

Siegel, Beatrice
    Cory: Corazon Aquino and the Philippines

    "Lodestar books."
    Bibliography: p.
    Includes index
    Summary: A biography of the political newcomer who ran for the office of president of the Philippines following her husband's assassination and defeated President Ferdinand Marcos in the 1986 election. Includes an interview with President Aquino.
        1. Aquino, Corazon Cojuangco—Juvenile literature.
    2. Philippines—Politics and government—1946-        —
    Juvenile literature.   3. Philippines—Presidents—
    Biography—Juvenile literature.   [1. Aquino, Corazon
    Cojuangco.   2. Philippines—Presidents]   I. Title.
    DS686.616.A65S54   1988   959.9′046′0924 [92]   87-24468
    ISBN 0-525-67235-4

Published in the United States by E. P. Dutton,
2 Park Avenue, New York, N.Y. 10016,
a division of NAL Penguin Inc.

Published simultaneously in Canada by
Fitzhenry & Whiteside Limited, Toronto

Editor: Virginia Buckley

Printed in the U.S.A.   W   First Edition
10 9 8 7 6 5 4 3 2 1

EKA 1

to Max and Marie

# Contents

# Acknowledgments

I would like to thank the many people who, in interviews and discussions, or in providing photographs, helped in the preparation of this book. Above all I would like to thank Imelda Nicolas, Assistant Appointment Secretary to President Aquino, and Luisa M. Howard for their generous assistance and advice. Also Elizabeth G. Advincula, Mary Rose Ezpeleta, Ramon Locsin, Mary Jo Mendoza, Anne Nelson, Sister Dora Sartino, Daniel B. Schirmer, Marion Solomon, Lino V. Tagle, and Michael Bedford. I would like to express special thanks to Dr. Federico Macaranas for his critical reading of the manuscript and his helpful comments.

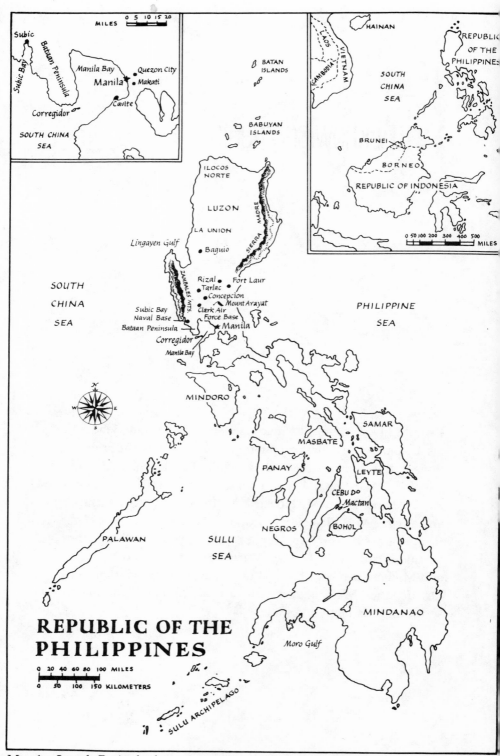

REPUBLIC OF THE PHILIPPINES

Map by Joseph P. Ascherl

# 1

# People Power

As far as the eye could see, the streets of Manila flowed like golden rivers. Tens of thousands of people wearing yellow T-shirts and hats, or carrying yellow flowers, moved in a solid mass as if drawn together by a magnet. Yellow ribbons, banners, and streamers waved and fluttered in the air. For this was election day, February 7, 1986, and yellow was the symbolic color of support for Corazon C. Aquino, who was running for president of the Philippines. She was the single candidate of a coalition of democratic forces and the first woman to run for presidential office in the Philippines.

Though Cory, as she was called, was a political newcomer, she was daring to challenge Ferdinand Marcos, who had held office for twenty years, nine of them under an official declaration of martial law. His military dictatorship had brought harsh years of repression in which there were sudden arrests, the

torture of political opponents, and the mysterious disappear-
ance of hundreds of activists. The country's economy had fallen
into such a severe decline that unemployment was widespread
and the poor worse off than ever. By contrast, a minority of
privileged government supporters lived in lavish splendor and
none more so than President Marcos and his wife, Imelda.

It was the hope of unseating Marcos that brought out the
largest number of voters in the country's history on this election
day. To reach one of 86,000 polling places throughout the
islands, people from far and wide traveled by ferry, car, boat,
horse and wagon, bus, and even by plane. Barefoot or in san-
dals, hundreds walked miles to their assigned voting booths.

Many doubted that the election would be honest. It was
common knowledge that the Marcos government controlled
polling places in the same way that it controlled the media and
the courts. Nor did people have confidence in the Commission
on Elections (COMELEC) appointed to oversee the voting. It
too was part of the Marcos network of political power.

As she crisscrossed the country during her campaign, Cory
Aquino carried with her a special mystique or aura. She per-
sonified the towering figure of her husband, Senator Benigno
Aquino, Jr., who had been assassinated in 1983 on his return
to the Philippines after three years of exile. He had come to
represent the most serious threat to the Marcos regime. Re-
sponsibility for his murder pointed to the government and its
military officers.

Like her murdered husband, Cory Aquino was putting her
life on the line when she faced Marcos loyalists and the armed
local warlords who controlled rural areas. She spoke in words
made famous by her husband, quoting his phrases as she tried
to bring alive his dream of a free and independent country. She
condemned all aspects of the Marcos dictatorship and insisted on "the inherent dignity and worth of every human being
. . . on freedom of thought and speech and press . . . and the

A show of support for President Corazon Aquino ROBERT
GUMPERT / THE GUARDIAN

liberty to choose . . . without fear or pressure—the public
officials of [one's] own choice . . ."

Under the slogan Peace and Reconciliation, she took her
message of freedom and social justice to every barrio, or small
village, from Luzon to Mindanao. She spoke from hastily
erected platforms in public squares, or from autos and backs of
trucks. She appealed to the poor and rich, to Catholics and
Muslims, to peasants and workers, to young and old. She identified in particular with the women who were so active in her
campaign, knowing how hard most of them had to struggle for
a living.

At first she spoke to small crowds. When her popularity increased, hundreds of people lined dusty country roads to see her while others waited in village squares. She saw their gradual awakening from years of passivity and fear as she became for them a symbol of hope, an angel bringing light to dark places. Because she had never held a government post, they saw her as pure, uncorrupted. Her slim figure and frank manner, her fresh face, unafraid, calm, made her compelling, beloved. The cry went up for "Cory! Cory! Cory!"

Not only had the election become an unfolding drama within the country, but the eyes of the world were on the Philippines. Tense events there dominated media headlines for the eighteen days from February 7, the day of the election, to the final unexpected climax February 25. Corazon Aquino's daring challenge to a long-entrenched military dictator was seen as a primal battle between good and evil.

In a country that was 80 percent Catholic, the Catholic church held great power. When the political contest heated up, the church made known its decision to remain neutral. Its refusal to support Marcos, who asked for its endorsement, opened the way for people to vote for Aquino. Eager to guarantee honest elections, the church sent volunteer poll watchers to voting places throughout the islands from a committee it supported, called the National Citizens' Movement for Free Elections (NAMFREL).

Though violence erupted all around Cory, it did not deter her from campaigning. Thugs fired into Aquino strongholds and attacked a motorcade in her hometown of Tarlac. Activist Aquino leaders were shot and killed.

Not only violence but dishonest voting practices were common despite the supervision of 50,000 volunteers. The Marcos machine used every stunt to guarantee victory. In a few rural areas, flying squads of Marcos supporters voted in two or three polling places. In others, voter lists were padded and nonexis-

A pro-Aquino rally on election day   ROBERTA FOSS/NAR-MIC/AFSC

tent voters cast ballots; actual voters were intimidated, bribed, and harassed.

The polling booths were open from 7:00 A.M. to 3:00 P.M. on Friday, February 7. Then the long official ballot counting began. By evening, despite incomplete returns, both sides claimed victory. Marcos, from his seat of power at Malacanang Palace in Manila, declared, "I probably won the election." Cory Aquino, learning of Marcos's statement, seized the moment and quickly announced that she was victorious. "The trend is clear and irreversible. The people and I have won and we know it," she said.

The results hung in the balance. Who had won the election? The counting of ballots continued for two days to widespread reports of fraud at the voting places. COMELEC, the government agency, continued to report that Marcos was elected whereas NAMFREL reported Cory Aquino in the lead.

On February 9, a startling event publicized the depth of government corruption. In Manila, about twenty-five computer operators walked out of the COMELEC tabulation center with computer disks and programs to confirm fraudulent counting reports. In other sections of the country, NAMFREL poll watchers, most of them women, carried ballot boxes out of polling places to safeguard them from Marcos goons. Coming to their aid, and protecting them from attack by Marcos police, were ordinary citizens and some members of the Reform Armed Forces Movement (RAM). Resistance to Marcos was expanding into unexpected quarters, attracting support from groups within the military.

Tensions mounted in street confrontations between Aquino and Marcos supporters, in shouting matches and fistfights. But on Thursday, February 13, the day Marcos chose for his official announcement of victory, the air was stilled with mass grief. On that day the body of a young Aquino supporter, Evelio Javier, killed by masked gunmen, was brought to Manila for public memorial services. He had been a graduate of Harvard's John F. Kennedy School of Government. Cory Aquino knew him well. Her presence at the funeral services turned the day of mourning into a mass protest against Marcos.

The next day, the Catholic Bishops Conference of the Philippines issued a statement. Condemning election fraud, they said their count of ballots placed Corazon Aquino ahead of Marcos by 600,000 votes. Clearly Corazon Aquino had won the election. But the Marcos government refused to concede defeat. To claim her victory, Cory Aquino called on the power of the people to assert itself against dictatorship.

On February 16, nine days after the election, a million people gathered in the Luneta, a public park in Manila. Aquino, bolstered by the mighty show of support, called for a national campaign of civil disobedience. She asked for a consumer boycott against all industries controlled by Marcos and urged continuous passive resistance.

The United States government, pressured to take a position on the Philippine election by several members of Congress, finally threatened Marcos with a cut in military and economic aid unless he acknowledged defeat. Still, Marcos continued to hold on to power.

The streets were taken over by people chanting "Cory! Cory! Cory!" in a tireless cry that continued even as Marcos threatened to send in the army to crack down on protesters. At this warning, the Catholic church called on civilians to protect its radio station, Veritas, from being seized, because its voice was the only source of news of the Aquino victory.

Support behind Aquino continued to broaden as the real extent of government election fraud became known. Leaders of big business, professionals, and members of the upper class came over to her side. When two long-entrenched government officials defected and announced support for Corazon Aquino, it triggered four days of revolutionary fervor that brought the situation to a head.

Defense Minister Juan Ponce Enrile and Deputy Chief of the Armed Forces Lieutenant General Fidel Ramos had been Marcos friends and supporters for many years. On Saturday, February 22, they confirmed at a press conference that there had been massive cheating in the election and that they were leaving the government. Enrile had contacted both United States Ambassador Stephen Bosworth and Cardinal Jaime Sin, the archbishop of Manila, asking for protection for themselves and those members of the armed forces who had defected with them.

Cardinal Jaime Sin   DAVID VITA

Cardinal Sin immediately went on the air, appealing to people to defend the two military camps where Enrile and Ramos were secluded. The cardinal's plea brought thousands of people to the camps. Women with children, men, students, workers, nuns in their habits poured onto the streets of Manila from

Young women, part of the human wall formed to protect Ramos and Enrile, hand flowers to a soldier.   JOHN CHUA

homes, schools, and factories to protect the defectors. They carried rosaries and flowers. They formed a human chain ferrying food and ammunition to the armed forces at the camps in preparation for an attack by the Marcos government. The massive civil disobedience movement had entered a militant stage that affirmed Cory Aquino's campaign statement "I hate to see what an angry people can do if you frustrate their will."

Determined to bring down the Marcos regime and claim their electoral victory, people willingly risked their lives. At the approach of a column of army tanks, they linked arms to form a human barricade; others lay down in the streets. They said, "You will not pass."

Unwilling to advance into a wall of people, the Marcos soldiers stopped their attack. They emerged from the tanks and reached out to the women, men, and children and took the flowers and food handed to them. They then returned to their tanks and backed away.

The historic events were shown on a television station to the millions of Aquino supporters and to Marcos supporters throughout the country.

Four days of mass action, the human barricades, the show of people power astonished not only the Marcos government but the whole world. In their determination to win the day, millions lost their fear and discovered their will to fight. They found the strength to topple a remorseless government that had jailed and murdered dissenters. They were urged on by their hope that the new president would remake the country, that at last they would be guaranteed a just life.

Though Marcos still held on to the reins of government, his time was up. The days became festive as support for Aquino continued to pour in from additional sections of the armed forces. The United Democratic Opposition party (UNIDO), which carried out the presidential campaign, announced over television the formation of a provisional government. Corazon Aquino, proclaiming her victory, led in the singing of the "Ave Maria," a universal prayer of the Catholic church.

On February 25, Corazon C. Aquino placed her left hand over a Bible held by her mother-in-law, Dona Aurora Aquino, and took the oath of office. She became the seventh president of the Philippines. Her running mate, Salvador Laurel, was sworn in as vice-president. Juan Ponce Enrile was named defense minister of the new government and Fidel Ramos became armed forces chief of staff.

One hour later, Ferdinand Marcos took the oath of office in ceremonies at Malacanang Palace. But behind closed doors, secret negotiations had been going on for Marcos to leave the country. On February 25, at 9:30 P.M., Marcos; his wife, Imelda; and close aides and friends, including his chief of staff,

General Fabian C. Ver, were flown to U.S. Clark Air Force Base en route to Hawaii.

During the next few days, revelers took over Malacanang Palace to see for themselves the lavish wastefulness of the dictator and his wife. Liberation day came, with celebrations and fireworks, dancing in the streets, prayer, and a chorus of voices. As thousands sang their favorite patriotic song, "Bayan Ko" ("My Country"), they put special emphasis on the last line: "To see you rise, forever free."

# 2

## Bayan Ko

Corazon Aquino had always been a good student, and she knew her country's history. She knew of its centuries of continuous unrest, and the martyrs and heroes who had inspired over four hundred years of struggle. It seemed to her that there had always been rebels hidden in mountain strongholds, leading the fight for national freedom.

The struggle started in the sixteenth century when Spain, dreaming of expanding its empire, sent conquistadores around the world. One of them was Ferdinand Magellan. Though Portuguese born, he sailed under the Spanish flag. During his great adventure to locate the Spice Islands and the riches of Asia, he led his ships and crew on a new course. He sailed west across the Atlantic Ocean and down around South America through what is now called the Strait of Magellan. After four months of barely moving over the becalmed Pacific Ocean, Magellan and his crew, continuing to sail west, dropped anchor at a chain of islands in 1521.

On one of the islands, Cebu, the people welcomed Magellan in the spirit of friendship. Magellan, however, had more than friendship in mind, for he was an emissary of a Christian world determined to spread its doctrine. In proper ceremonies, Magellan had eight hundred natives baptized into the Roman Catholic religion.

Encouraged by his easy success, he sailed south to the island of Mactan. There he did not receive the same courteous treatment. Not only did the island chieftain refuse to pay ceremonial and financial tribute to Magellan, but he called on his people to repel the invaders. They mounted a bloody skirmish, using spears, stones, and arrows against more advanced foreign weapons. In hand-to-hand fighting, Magellan and seven or eight seamen were killed. The others, to escape attack, fled back to their big ships and sailed away.

A determined Spain sent Miguel Lopez de Legaspi from Spanish Mexico in 1564 to complete the conquest. He succeeded in establishing a settlement on the island of Cebu. From that foothold, Spain spread control over the other islands.

Through its invasion, Spain gained an archipelago made up of 7,100 islands stretched out along the western edge of the Pacific Ocean. The islands vary in size from nameless reefs jutting out of the ocean at low tide to large land masses such as Luzon in the north and Mindanao in the south. Of the thousands of islands, eleven account for 96 percent of the land.

The islands, thought to have broken away eons ago from the Asian continent in a volcanic upheaval, share with the mainland the turmoil of earthquakes, active volcanoes, and frequent typhoons. The terrain of fertile plains and mountain peaks is also similar to the mainland's, as is the tropical climate. The islands go through rainless months when blazing sun scorches the earth. In other months monsoon winds and drenching rains buffet the coastal regions.

Natives on Mactan battle Magellan and the Spanish invaders.

Spain named the islands the Philippines after its king Philip II and, hoping to discover great riches, as it had in Mexico, it sent native work gangs into mines to dig for deposits of gold. Disappointed that no treasure was found, the Spanish nevertheless considered the islands valuable. They were a stepping stone to the products of the fabled East, to silks, porcelains, jewels, and spices. Equally important was the islands' role as a base of operations for missionary work to other Asian countries. In this role, Catholic friars became a major instrument of Spanish influence and colonial rule.

In their zeal to win converts, the friars spread out into the heart of the islands, into the *barangays,* or family kinship units. They found a people generally of Malay origin divided into distinct groups. Each group spoke its own language, built its own villages, and was different and independent of the others. Though the native people subsisted by hunting, gathering, farming, and fishing, fish was plentiful and became the basic

An ancient agricultural technique survives—rice fields terraced
into the hills. PHILIPPINE MINISTRY OF TOURISM

food. To be near the food supply, they became a coastal people
living on the edge of the sea or on the banks of rivers. And to
avoid the dangers of seasonal flooding, they built houses on
stilts. Moreover, villagers traveled by water, up and down rivers
and along the coast, carrying on a modest trade with one another and with visiting Asian merchants and seamen.

No federation or political unity bound the groups together.
Precisely this lack of unity made it easy for the Catholic church
to win converts and control. Only in the south, on Mindanao
and Sulu, where the Muslim Moros clung to the faith of their
Islamic ancestors, was Spain defeated in its conquest. The Muslims remained not only free of Spain but often raided the colonial settlements.

Over the years, the friars bought tracts of land for the church,

Mosques, *above,* and sailing vessels, *below,* reflect Muslim culture in the southern Philippines. PHILIPPINE MINISTRY OF TOURISM

developing them into huge haciendas, or plantations. The friars collected taxes and employed labor, most of it free, and they baptized and converted, making the Philippines the only Christian nation in Asia.

Spain ruled the islands with a heavy hand through an appointed governor-general. To encourage settlers, he handed out royal grants, or *encomiendas,* as they were called. These grants gave settlers administrative control over a piece of land and its native inhabitants, from whom they could collect taxes and demand forced labor. In return the settlers had certain responsibilities: to protect the native people, support the Catholic missionaries, and help defend the colony.

Forced labor had built Manila, on the island of Luzon, into a walled fortress-city within which were government buildings, a huge cathedral, churches, and a public square. The city was also the commercial center, a marketplace for foreign products. The world of commerce found its way to the Philippines through the Spanish galleons. These huge, square-rigged vessels sailed into the port of Manila, connecting the Philippines to Spanish Mexico and to South China for the important China trade.

Within the city lived the Spanish colonialists, who used the native population to supply them with food and services. To supervise native labor, a new group of native elite, or *principales,* emerged. They acted as intermediaries between the Spanish conquerors and the people. In practice they became the brutal overseers of labor, in return for which they received privileges such as tax exemptions, special titles, and the right to exploit *Indio* labor on their own behalf.

By the eighteenth and nineteenth centuries, waves of Chinese had settled on the islands, blending their skills into the culture. A new mix of people and a new social structure developed. By the end of the nineteenth century, economic wealth was concentrated in the hands of upper-class Spanish and Chinese. Below them were the *mestizos,* children of islanders who had intermarried with either the Spanish or Chinese. Then came the *principales,* or elite islanders. In the lowest and poorest class were the *Indios,* the pure islanders, those who carried the burden of town and rural labor. They were the landless, forced to work countless hours in the tropical heat. Underfed and exhausted, they died by the thousands. To escape brutal lives, many fled to the hills to join resistance groups and the non-Christian people.

The history of the Philippines moved in two directions: The native upper class, or elite, accommodated to the demands of Spanish authority and became oppressors themselves. At the same time, resistance to foreign domination developed among the poor and the newly educated. Each generation produced leaders who inspired the fight for freedom.

Forms of resistance varied. There were subtle ways of holding on to native culture. While giving lip service to Catholicism, native priests led villagers in the practice of their old religion and in rituals connected to the worship of nature spirits. These practices often existed in addition to attendance at church.

Some villagers became refugees from Spanish-dominated land and converted to Islam, joining the Moros in attacks on Spanish strongholds.

The most overt form of resistance was armed rebellion. Brutal repression of uprisings spawned more rebellion, especially among the Tagalog and Pampanga people north of Manila. On the island of Bohol, in the central part of the country, uprisings disrupted Spanish rule for eighty-five years, from 1744 to 1829.

Discontent simmered on one island or another, making the friars and military wary of every public meeting and local protest. Often they saw armed rebellion where there was none. They were especially alert to the talk of a newly educated class of Filipinos who, studying abroad, returned with liberal ideas of government.

Because of the fears of the ruling class, a minor incident

escalated into a revolutionary upsurge. The incident happened in Cavite, south of Manila, in 1872. Two hundred Filipino soldiers at the Spanish military barracks staged an uprising to protest the loss of privileges, their exemption from forced labor and payment of tribute. Though the protest was a local issue, the Spanish governor-general used it as an excuse to crush the growing spirit of discontent, and he let loose a reign of terror in which forty-one people were executed and thousands were sentenced to life in jail. Three innocent priests were among those cruelly put to death in the public square at Cavite. The brutality horrified the country and galvanized protest into revolutionary channels. The year 1872 marked a turning point, and the beginning of the revolutionary movement for independence from Spain—for nationhood.

The movement included both reform and radical leaders. One of the great propagandists of the time was Jose Rizal. Like many others, he had studied in Spain and France and returned with new ideas of a social order. He was a brilliant scholar, writer, and educator, and had organized a group called La Liga Filipina. He saw the league as a reform organization, a form of mutual aid society that would prod the government and church to change and provide basic liberties.

Andres Bonifacio was a different kind of leader. Of simple birth but both bold and learned, he formed a secret society called the Katipunan, or Sons of the People, shortened from the full Tagalog name meaning Supreme and Most Honorable Association of the Sons of the Motherland. Under its banner, this rebel group vowed to overthrow Spanish rule.

Both leaders became martyrs in the fight for freedom. Rizal was executed by a government firing squad in 1896. Bonifacio lost his life in a power struggle with another faction led by a newcomer, Emilio Aguinaldo, a small landowner.

The outrageous executions and killings fired the spirit of the rebels and gave momentum to the revolutionary movement.

Dr. Jose Rizal, *left,* and Andres Bonifacio, *right*  NATIONAL
HISTORICAL INSTITUTE, MANILA

Growing forces demanded complete independence for the Philippines. Borrowing from the French revolution, the rebels
adopted the slogan Liberty, Equality, and Fraternity.

By 1896, heavy fighting had broken out between rebel groups
led by Aguinaldo and the Spanish military. Though the Filipinos were becoming expert in guerrilla warfare, especially the
sudden skirmish and fast retreat into the mountains, they
nevertheless suffered heavy losses. To bring peace to the country, Aguinaldo was forced to agree to a truce and to go into exile
in return for a written guarantee of reforms. The reforms were
never granted, and in February 1898, the revolution again
erupted and spread through the country. Heavy fighting took
place north of Manila in Tarlac and Pampanga, and south on
the islands of Cebu and Panay.

Emilio Aguinaldo THE LIBRARY OF CONGRESS

The rebels were close to defeating Spain. They could feel their victory. Unforeseen was the ambition of the United States, considered a friend by the rebels.

In 1898, Theodore Roosevelt was assistant secretary of the navy under President William McKinley. Roosevelt claimed it was the destiny of the United States to become a great power. Along with other officials who shared his ambition, he planned his strategy in advance. When the United States declared war against Spain in April 1898, over the issue of Cuba, Theodore Roosevelt set into motion his secret maneuvers. He ordered the United States fleet under Commodore George Dewey to sail

Admiral George Dewey, 1899   OFFICIAL U.S. NAVY PHOTO-
GRAPH

from its base in Hong Kong to Manila. On May 1, Dewey sailed
into Manila Bay and in a swift battle defeated the decrepit
Spanish fleet without the loss of a single American life.

In the meantime, the rebel Philippine army had marched into
Manila and sacked the city. They were victorious and had won
their freedom. On June 12, 1898, in the town of Cavite, they
issued a constitution and announced the establishment of the
first Philippine republic, with Aguinaldo as president. Their
constitution, based on that of the United States, granted basic
democratic rights.

That same month, United States military forces landed in

Manila. In secret negotiations, the United States government arranged for a defeated Spain to surrender—not to the Philippine rebel army—but to the U.S. military. In a treaty signed in Paris in December 1898, Spain officially ceded the Philippines to the United States.

Despite heated debate and public protest, the United States Congress, on February 4, 1899, approved the treaty and annexation of the Philippines. By April that year, the United States made its intentions clear to the world in the Schurman Commission report: "The supremacy of the United States must and will be enforced throughout every part of the Archipelago [the Philippines] and those who resist it can accomplish no end other than their own ruin."

The betrayal of the Philippine revolution brought into action a new guerrilla movement—this one against the United States. Hidden in mountain ranges and hills were men and women who continued to battle the United States military for seven years despite an official surrender in 1902. By 1906, a weary country that had lost an estimated 500,000 to the fight against the new invaders was finally subdued. The United States had thought it would quietly take over the Philippines, but it had done so only with repeated increases in military strength and armaments and the loss of 10,000 soldiers.

Under the first U.S.–appointed civil governor, William Howard Taft, the United States established its apparatus for colonial domination of more than seven million people. At that time, 90 percent of the population was Christian; Muslim and other minorities made up the remaining 10 percent.

The economy and agriculture took on new life. The countryside was opened up to cattle ranching, while peasants converted jungles into farmland. They did not become landowners but remained dependent on a new set of powerful landlords and entrepreneurs. In the land grabbing, a handful of Spanish, Americans, and Chinese became rich.

To give the Philippines some benefits of a benign foreign rule, the United States built schools and hospitals, repaired roads, and dug cisterns for water. It opened health clinics, and by 1908 had built the University of the Philippines. A free system of education increased the literacy level of the general population.

At the same time, United States culture and its values permeated the islands, especially the cities. English became the required language in business and diplomacy; school children sang songs in English and not in their native languages. Large feudal estates were left intact while the country was made profitable for United States investors. Above all, the islands became both a source of raw products and a market for U.S.–manufactured products. Not to be overlooked were the advantages to the United States of establishing a military presence and power base in the Pacific, close to mainland China and the routes to the Middle East.

# 3

# East and West

When Maria Corazon, the fourth of six children, was born into the Cojuangco family on January 25, 1933, the Philippine Islands were still a colony of the United States. But the United States was beginning to loosen its colonial grip, and in 1934, the Tydings-McDuffie act provided for the establishment of a Philippine commonwealth, and in 1935, Manuel Quezon was elected its first president. The act also provided for complete Philippine independence in 1946, if the country "learned how to govern itself."

Cory, as she was called from childhood, grew up in two worlds: the Philippines, or the world of the East, in which she was born and raised; and the United States, or the world of the West, in which she was educated.

Cory's father, Jose Cojuangco, was of Chinese ancestry and

had been reared in the province of Tarlac. There his family started out as small mill owners and became, over the years, *hacenderos,* or large landowners, of sugar plantations. Her mother, Demetria Sumulong, with family roots in Indo-Malay stock, grew up in Rizal in a family distinguished for its education and other achievements. Cory remembers her father as easygoing and her mother as the family disciplinarian. Her mother instilled in the children her deep Catholic faith, a sense of modesty and thrift, and the need for education and good work. *Ora et Labora,* Pray and Work, was her motto.

The great landowning and banking wealth of Cory's family placed them high among the Philippine elite. Because of their wealth and political involvements, they were among those who influenced the country's decisions. During Cory's growing-up years, her father and brother were congressmen, and her maternal grandfather, Juan Sumulong, and an uncle served in the senate.

The upper class, in accommodating to their country's colonial status, became the link between the Philippines and the United States. They formed a bridge to the Western world, in which they felt at home.

The Americanization of the Philippines created western-style cities throughout the islands. Products manufactured in the United States, from plastics to blue jeans, could be found in markets and stores. Manila, in particular, became a replica of the West. It was a city of neon lights, discos, Hollywood movies, pop music, and designer shops. For Cory, who had absorbed the ethics of her mother's teaching, the fast-paced life was forbidden. There were no shopping sprees in chic boutiques, no sleek automobiles, no wild parties. Always properly chaperoned, she was more the refined upper-class young woman who wore gloves and a hat when visiting or having tea.

Her wealth and privilege also isolated her from the upheavals in city and countryside. Unknown to her was the squalor of the poor, the fact that children often were hungry, dying of starva-

A busy street in downtown Manila   UN PHOTO

tion. She knew little of peasant uprisings and working-class strikes.

From her upper-class home, Cory went to Manila's exclusive convent schools to start her education. At age six, she entered the grade school of Saint Scholastica's College, where she was a quiet little girl who diligently did her homework.

In 1942, when she was nine years old, Japan invaded her country and occupied Manila. She remembers that she had to sing songs in the Japanese tongue, Nippongo. She also remembers that at the end of 1944, when she was eleven, the United States started its reconquest of her country, and in the heavy bombing, her home was shattered and her school damaged. Like other families, hers too moved from one house to another to avoid the terrible air raids. For her first year of high school, she transferred to Assumption Convent School.

World War II left Manila destroyed and gutted, its educational facilities in ruins. One million people, out of a population of 20 million, lost their lives, including women and children, but mostly the young men of draft age.

Right after the war, Jose Cojuangco, to serve his banking interests, moved the family to the United States. They settled in Philadelphia, Pennsylvania, and for her high school sophomore year, Cory became a boarding-school student at the exclusive Ravenhill Academy. When her parents returned to Manila, Cory, an older sister, and two cousins stayed on in the United States to continue their education. The Western world would become Cory's second home.

From 1947 to 1949, she was a student at the small Notre Dame Convent School on Manhattan's west side. In two turn-of-the-century brownstones put together into classrooms, offices, and a convent, Corazon Aquino deepened her Catholic faith and continued her excellent scholarship. She is remembered by classmates as a petite youngster who was gentle and friendly and who seemed self-contained, as if she moved along on her own inner force. Not noted in any way for leadership, she was nevertheless very much a part of the school and its clubs and entertainments.

In her Prediction for the Future, written for the 1949 Notre Dame yearbook, might be glimpsed the basis of Cory's fortitude. She wrote, "It is up to you to bring to the life you are entering, to the state you must help to form, an energy of true religious faith."

From Notre Dame, Cory went on to a woman's Catholic college in Riverdale, New York. Mount Saint Vincent, located on a tree-lined campus of seventy acres overlooking the Hudson River, was a small college of five hundred students. In its tranquil setting, Cory matured into young womanhood.

There, too, she was a good student, taking honors in French and math, and elected secretary of the history and cultural club, Epsilon Phi. As in her other schools, students recall her as quiet, friendly, a "bookish type," someone who did not "make

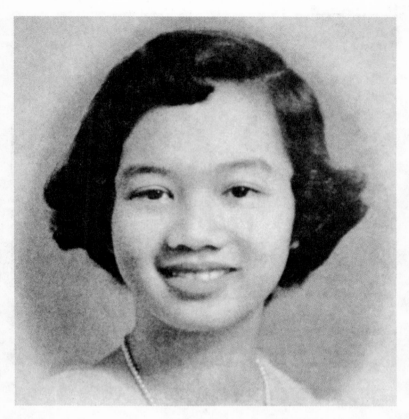

Corazon Cojuangco, 1949, at the Notre Dame Convent School, New York City

a stir." A few have an image of Cory tagging along after her older sister, Teresita, a student in the class before hers. Others recall the fun of an annual Festival of Nations program when Cory, Teresita, and two other Filipino students, costumed in traditional dress with puffed-out sleeves, did a folk dance called *tinikling.*

In each of the U.S. schools Cory attended, she was essentially an outsider, a member of a tiny group of students of Asian origin. Yet she was always comfortable. A feeling of acceptance came naturally with her upper-class status. She was accustomed to mixing with the wealthy and influential. Equally im-

The Administration Building of the College of Mount Saint Vincent

portant was her tie to Catholic school students and faculty, with whom she shared a strong religious faith, a faith that would be the mainstay of her life. There were also Cory's bright intelligence and other gifts contributing to her self-confidence. By the third year of college, she was a pretty young woman with a willowy figure and a very bright mind.

During her seven years of schooling abroad, Cory flew home for holidays and vacations. On one home visit during her last year at college, she became reacquainted with Benigno Aquino, Jr., whom she had known as a child. They had both grown up in the province of Tarlac, north of Manila. Cory's family were large landowners in the town of Tarlac itself. Not far from them, in the town of Concepcion, the Aquino family, too, were *hacenderos.* Cory knew Ninoy, as Benigno, Jr., was called, to be a bright, vivid youngster who always had a gift for the spoken word.

On her visit home in her senior year, Ninoy began to date her. Though only twenty-one, he already had a reputation as the boy wonder of Manila. Four years before, a teenager and inexperienced in journalism, he had talked his way into a job as a foreign correspondent for the *Manila Times,* to cover the Korean War (1950–1953). He learned his skills on the job, sending back stories from the battlefront, describing the terrible tragedies of death and violence. His experiences changed him, and his reports gave readers a realistic account of the war.

When Cory had met him in previous years at parties, she always considered him too talkative and self-centered; he was actually "dull," she thought. But on getting to know him again in 1952, she discovered a new Ninoy. This time he interested her. She found him intelligent, dynamic, and articulate, "easy to talk to." And, to her surprise, he was quite mature.

After her return to college, she and Ninoy wrote to each other regularly. His love letters impressed her, she would remark. "Not mush, for one thing," she said.

At age twenty, and having graduated from college, Cory returned to Manila and enrolled in the Far Eastern University to study law. Her maternal grandfather, Juan Sumulong, had been one of the most brilliant jurists of his time, serving on the negotiating committee to win commonwealth status for the Philippines. Cory, however, did not plan to follow in his footsteps. She thought of law as a discipline rather than a career. As it turned out, she spent most of her time with Ninoy. He too was a law student, at the Ateneo, a Jesuit school in Manila.

The two young people were by now deeply in love and the talk of their social set: Cory Cojuangco and Ninoy Aquino. He was an attentive suitor, escorting Cory to dances, to the movies, and to church. Early in the courtship, he tried to persuade her to marry him. But Cory was cautious and wanted to be sure they really liked each other. "Not yet," she would say. "I don't think this is the right time." Though both sets of parents encouraged the marriage and urged a brief engagement, they made it clear that they wanted Ninoy to finish law school.

Ninoy won out. Cory dropped out of law school at the end of the first semester, and on October 11, 1954, she and Ninoy were married in the parish church Our Lady of Sorrows. For her wedding Cory was gowned in white nylon tulle, with pearled silk banding on the bouffant skirt. The morning wedding was attended by the elite of the Philippines, including its president, Ramon Magsaysay. Right after the wedding breakfast at the Manila Hotel, Ninoy and Cory left on their honeymoon. Their destination was the United States, where Ninoy had been assigned by the Philippine president for a four-month stint to observe training methods in the United States intelligence schools.

In February 1955, Cory and Ninoy returned home. Though Ninoy had only to complete the fourth year of law school, he dropped out for good. Now that he was married, he said, he had to think of his family.

He left the sights and sounds of Manila, bought land in his home town of Concepcion, and embarked on the life of a farmer. He said good-bye to law, to journalism, to serving on honored presidential committees.

But buying land in Concepcion was really the first step in a political career.

# 4

# The Aquino Family

Ninoy Aquino did not have to look far to understand why he was drawn to politics. He was continuing the legacy handed down by his grandfather and father. They both had deep roots in Philippine nationalism and believed in the right of people to shape their lives and country in their own way. In a sense their nationalism stemmed from a personal affront that educated, wealthy people had to take orders from a colonial power. In their passionate fight for independence, Ninoy's grandfather and father had been pursued, imprisoned, and exiled.

Ninoy's landowning family had long ago settled in the town of Concepcion. Their plantation was one of many rice and sugarcane fields that stretched north and south through the central plain of Luzon. The land was made rich and fertile by a network of rivers that wound through the fields. On either side of the valley rose mountain chains. On the west were the Zambales

Water buffalo, *above,* are used by farmers; workmen, *below,* gather coconuts for husking.   UN PHOTOS

A young boy rides a water buffalo.   OFFICIAL U.S. NAVY PHO-
TOGRAPH

and on the east the Sierra Madre. For hundreds of years the dense mountain forests had been sanctuaries for successive groups of resistance fighters. Dominating the plain at the southern tip was another guerrilla hideout, Mount Arayat, casting giant shadows over the countryside from its height of over one thousand feet.

In Mount Arayat, Ninoy's grandfather, Servillano Aquino, hid with five hundred of his crack troops during the fight against Spain at the turn of the century. He was a devoted follower of the guerrilla leader, Aguinaldo, in whose rebel army he became a general.

Captured by Spanish forces, Servillano was thrown into jail, tried in a military court, and sentenced to death before a firing squad. His execution was to take place in three days. When his two oldest sons, one of them Ninoy's father, visited him in prison, they found him thin and pale but ready for execution.

In a general amnesty declared by the government, Servillano's life was spared. Immediately upon being let out of jail, he exiled himself to Hong Kong, to be near his leader, Aguinaldo.

The betrayal of the Philippine revolution by the United States in 1898 stunned Servillano. He joined Aguinaldo in a new revolutionary army, this one against the United States. Again he was captured and court-martialed, this time by the United States army, which condemned him to jail for life.

After four years, Servillano was released from jail, and he returned to his land and life as a *hacendero* in Concepcion. Throughout his lifetime he remained an outspoken opponent of the foreign occupation of his country. Often he would boast that he had been a prisoner of the Americans! And scornful of the rich Filipinos who worshiped everything American, he refused to learn English and spoke only his native tongue.

He was a powerful family figure, fearless and independent in his thinking. His sons revered him. His grandson, Ninoy, scoffed at such reverence and quipped when his grandfather

Philippine independence soldiers, about 1900, who fought U.S. troops

visited, "The Emperor has arrived." Of course Ninoy adored his grandfather as he did his own father, Benigno Aquino, Sr.

Ninoy, born in Concepcion on November 27, 1932, was named after both these men, Benigno Servillano Aquino, Jr. His father was also a powerful man. He had been a brilliant scholar and lawyer who settled in Concepcion. On his marriage he built his own home near his father and called it Hacienda Tinang. Ninoy, a child of Benigno's second marriage to Dona Aurora, grew up in a family that lived and breathed politics, love of country, and hatred of colonial domination. In his growing-up years, Ninoy knew his father as a congressman and then a senator. His father was only thirty-eight years old when Manuel Quezon, the first Philippine president under the commonwealth, appointed him to a cabinet post. To celebrate the honor, the Aquinos had an auditorium built for a gala that drew 5,000 of the island's elite.

On December 7, 1941, World War II shattered the peace in the Pacific Basin. The Japanese bombing of the U.S. fleet at Pearl Harbor in Hawaii was followed ten hours later with a crippling blow to the U.S. fleet stationed in the Philippines. To spare Manila from destruction, the government declared that it would not be defended against invasion—it would be an open city.

Throughout the following weeks, the Japanese continued their punishing assault, landing troops in the Lingayen Gulf of Luzon. Under General Douglas MacArthur, in charge of Philippine–United States defenses, the Philippine government was removed to the fortified island of Corregidor off Bataan Peninsula, where soldiers fought to guard the entrance to Manila Bay. Eighty thousand troops, four-fifths of them Filipino, battled the Japanese to prevent an invasion. When General MacArthur fled with his aides to Australia, to direct the Pacific war effort from a safe place, U.S.–Filipino troops, under Lieutenant General Jonathan M. Wainwright, continued to defend Bataan. Finally forced to surrender, more than 30,000 troops were taken prisoner, lined up, and marched under the blazing sun to concentration camps forty miles away. Fifteen thousand soldiers perished from their wounds or exhaustion. The route became known as the Bataan Death March.

The military defeat and the flight of U.S. forces left many islanders feeling abandoned by the United States. They considered the death of thousands at Bataan a futile show of resistance. In May 1942, after continuous heavy bombardments, the Japanese annexed the Philippine Islands.

Ninoy's father was one of those who raged against the needless deaths at Bataan. President Quezon, too, felt his country was left to burn and die needlessly. Both Quezon and his vice-president, Sergio Osmena, escaped to the United States, where they set up a government in exile.

The Japanese invasion into the central plains of Luzon and other islands was brutal. Japanese soldiers looted, raped, burned, and killed on their march through the barrios. To protect homes and families, a new Filipino resistance army developed. Men and women who saw their country destroyed by the invaders took to the hills once again. In central Luzon the major guerrilla fighters were called the Huks, short for Hukbalahap, a Tagalog phrase meaning People's Anti-Japanese Army. Among the first leaders was a woman, Felipa Culala, who helped make the guerrilla fight peasant-based. Under the leadership of Luis Taruc, a known communist, the Huks developed into a dedicated anti-Japanese fighting force that attracted not only peasants but students, the clergy, professionals, and many of the upper class, all determined to repel the Japanese. At its height, the Huk movement had an army of 30,000. But there were other anti-Japanese forces, and before the war was over, more than 200,000 guerrillas were attacking Japanese positions.

Once again the country was polarized: On the one hand, there was the growing resistance movement; on the other, accommodation to the Japanese by large segments of the elite.

Among those who supported the Japanese and became part of the Japanese puppet government was Ninoy's father, Benigno Aquino, Sr. He was so impatient for immediate Philippine independence that he believed the Japanese promise of full freedom for his country. And conscious of the Malay origin of his people, he called himself an Orientalist and said, "We belong to the East."

On October 14, 1943, the Japanese established a nominally independent Philippine republic, at the head of which was Jose P. Laurel as president. It turned out to be a gesture by which the Japanese hoped to subdue the people. But Benigno Aquino, Sr., took it upon himself to travel through the islands to address crowded audiences and convince them of Japan's good intentions. On many occasions, however, he secretly interceded with the Japanese to protest their brutality.

It was a terrible time for many Filipinos, who did not know

which side to support when they saw distinguished leaders become collaborators of the Japanese. Many asked whether it mattered which country dominated them.

By mid 1944, United States armed forces stationed on other Pacific islands had regrouped, rearmed, and were prepared to reconquer the Philippines. After a month of continuous air strikes against Japanese installations, the first liberation army, led by General MacArthur, landed at Leyte on October 20, 1944. During the next few days, one of the heaviest naval battles of all time took place between the United States fleet and the Japanese. By January 1945, troops landed on the island of Luzon; in the following month, the city of Manila was retaken, and by July 1945, the whole island was liberated. In the fierce fighting, the land was devastated, the economy destroyed, and the country torn by political turmoil. Manila, reduced to ruins, was one of the worst-bombed cities of World War II.

At the onset of the United States military invasion, Ninoy's father and others of the puppet government fled to Tokyo for safety. He was not safe, however, from the arm of the United States military police. By the end of the war, the United States also occupied Japan. Orders were carried out to arrest Benigno Aquino, Sr., and place him in jail. Poor prison conditions weakened his health, and he suffered a heart attack and ministrokes.

The contradictions of the times did not go unnoted. Aquino was still in a Tokyo jail when presidential elections in the Philippines were called in April 1946. The man who won office was Manuel Roxas, a close friend of General MacArthur. Roxas was known as a Japanese collaborator. But MacArthur cleared his record, claiming he had been secretly providing information to United States intelligence. Most important, Roxas could be counted on to watch over United States interests in the Philippines.

On July 4, 1946, the United States granted the Philippine Islands their independence. The wild festivities celebrating this event did not reach Aquino in his Tokyo jail.

But six weeks after independence, in August 1946, he and his colleagues were flown back home to a local prison, where he at long last had a reunion with his family. At his trial a month later, he pleaded innocent to charges of treason and was released from jail. He went back home to Dona Aurora and his family in Concepcion. They defended him, claiming that he, like Roxas, had supplied the anti-Japanese armies with intelligence reports about troop movements.

Whatever the point of view, Ninoy suffered years of confusion over his father's wartime role. Shunned by friends, Ninoy became a loner, trying to sort out the facts. In the complexities of colonial politics, however, the line between treason and patriotism is not always clear, and the animosity toward the Aquino family lessened after the war. When Ninoy's father died suddenly of a heart attack on December 20, 1947, at age fifty-three, he was given full state honors at his burial, and the Philippine congress paid him tribute. Four days after his death, the case of treason against him was dismissed by the court.

Though the Philippine Islands had gained independence in 1946, to his last days, Benigno Aquino, Sr., and his father, Servillano, protested the continued foreign domination of their country. The Philippines, they said, had gained independence in name only but remained tied economically and militarily to the United States.

And indeed, at the time of independence, the government under Roxas had granted the United States a ninety-nine-year lease on army and naval bases, along with supervision over the building of a new Philippine army. A trade agreement gave special privileges to American investors, who would get equal rights with native industrialists in exploring and developing the island's economic resources.

# 5

# Political Beginnings

Cory had always considered the possibility that Ninoy would enter politics but not in the first year of their marriage. Her eyes were still blurred with visions of love and romance, of seeing her husband every evening at the end of a work day. But a new reality set in after Ninoy purchased land in Concepcion. He spent mid-week on the farm, cutting back the forests and jungle and joined her only on weekends in Manila. She was living with her mother-in-law at the large Aquino home, awaiting the birth of their first child.

Though Cory's preference was for the excitement of a large city, she could see settling in Concepcion as a way of putting down roots in a community in which to raise a family. Like Ninoy, she had grown up in a landowning family that had always maintained a home in Manila. Not only did Cory's family own land, but it was one of the wealthiest on the island.

Benigno Servillano Aquino, Jr.  PRESS OFFICE, MANILA

She was quite familiar with the comforts of upper-class life on a plantation and its traditional events centered around church, peasants, and a village square.

Ninoy had bought the acreage on the advice of Cory's father. His grandfather Servillano Aquino taught him how to put in an irrigation system. He also initiated Ninoy into the intricate practice of being a paternalistic farmer, one who dealt with the peasants on a basis of reciprocal obligation. The peasants worked the land, in return for which they had their basic needs taken care of by the landowner. In addition they owned a small plot of land and its produce. For Ninoy, who had a natural love for people, it was easy to be a concerned farmer.

The land presented more complex problems than relationships with the peasants. It bordered the province of Nueva Ecija, where enclaves of Huks and supporters controlled rural areas. During World War II, the Huks were a guerrilla group fighting the Japanese invasion. They changed their orientation after the war and became a tightly knit revolutionary organization, now called the People's Liberation Army. Their base was central Luzon, the hub of peasant unrest, where they led successful uprisings against the worst abuses of rural exploitation. By the early 1950s they were welded into an armed force of 15,000 to 20,000, despite repeated government military attacks to wipe them out. Every peasant protest was immediately labeled communist or Huk, though this was often not the case.

Ninoy Aquino knew the Huks very well, not only because he grew up in central Luzon but also because he had undertaken a special mission in 1954 for President Magsaysay. Even before his presidency, Magsaysay had directed his energy to weaken Huk influence. He had formulated programs that offered amnesty and relocation to Huks who came down from the hills. He also established a Filipino Rural Reconstruction organization, resembling the U.S. Peace Corps formed some years later. College students were sent into rural areas to live with the peasants, teach improved farming methods, set up health clinics, and start a literacy campaign.

The leader of the Huks, Luis Taruc, acknowledged that these tactics, as well as government efforts at general reform, had weakened his army of supporters, that his movement was on the decline. In 1954, Taruc let it be known that he was willing, under certain conditions, to surrender.

The man President Magsaysay sent into the mountains to locate and arrange for the surrender of Luis Taruc in May 1954 was twenty-one-year-old Ninoy Aquino. Notwithstanding Taruc's reputation as a dreaded communist, and the Huks as a cruel fighting force, Ninoy undertook the mission. He brought Taruc down from the mountains and handed him over to the government. Despite a promise of leniency, Taruc was put in jail, an act that enraged Ninoy Aquino and for which he held the government responsible. His successful mission enhanced his reputation, but he also became known as a friend of the communists and "a Huk lover," though at no time did he ever share their political philosophy.

Though Taruc had surrendered, active Huk enclaves continued their attacks because the abuses they addressed remained entrenched. The fundamental need, according to them, was for radical change: change that would once and for all divide the huge church and private estates among the landless peasants, bring an end to military violence and corruption, lower the horrendous usury charges for loans, and make updated farm machinery available. Only fundamental changes, they claimed, could improve the lives of the poor and end hunger in the countryside.

Ninoy Aquino, clearing his land in Huk territory, kept an eye out for them. He let it be known that he barricaded himself into his country shack at night with a shotgun and automatic rifle handy. The Huks, needless to say, did not bother him.

Finally, after the birth of their first child, a girl they named Maria Elena but would call Ballsy, Cory moved to Concepcion, where Ninoy was now planting rice on the farm. In the months that Cory had lived in Manila, Ninoy had learned to enjoy the company of the peasants with whom he ate and lived. He understood their problems and was therefore receptive to President Magsaysay's urging that he run for mayor of Concepcion.

Like Ninoy, Cory grew up in a family dominated by political talk. Both her father and brother held office, but more exciting were the campaigns for national office of her maternal grandfather, Senator Juan Sumulong. In 1935, he was a candidate for

vice-president in the country's first election under commonwealth status. In 1941, he ran for president against the incum-
bent Manuel Quezon. Though defeated in both races, Juan
Sumulong's career as jurist and politician was revered in Cory's
home.

What was missing in Cory's branch of the family was the
Aquino passion, the "give me liberty or give me death" quality
of life. She would get that from Ninoy. That passion ran in his
blood. He was fearless, dramatic, spoke his mind; he was a man
who would never beg for mercy.

He started out low-key, on the first rung of the political
ladder in 1955 when he became a candidate for mayor of Concepcion. In a three-way race, he held a centrist position, com-
peting with a conservative and a Huk supporter.

To help in the campaign, Cory moved into their new home
in Concepcion and soon learned her first lessons in practical
politics. Her house, she found, was no longer a private place but
open to the public. Neighbors freely dropped in at all hours to
give her unsolicited advice. They taught her how to cook on a
clay stove and how to diaper and care for her baby. Though
surprised at having to be in the public eye, the twenty-two-year-
old Cory Aquino reacted gracefully to the friendly overtures.
When she accompanied Ninoy to their farm near Nueva Ecija,
more surprises were in store, especially the rough living conditions. She was embarrassed when strange men lifted her up and
carried her over mud holes, or when she had to urinate in a tin
can because of the lack of bathroom facilities.

Cory told herself she had to learn the ropes, so she closely
observed her mother-in-law, Dona Aurora, on the campaign
trail. Here was a seasoned worker who had long years of experience as the wife of a politician. Cory noticed the way Dona
Aurora spoke to people in their native language, Pampango.
She also knew whom to seek out and what to talk about.

Cory was learning more fundamental things, that marriage

to Ninoy meant living in an atmosphere continuously charged with bolts of energy. Her husband was restless, a young man always on the go. Cory held on to her inner sense of peace and reserve but made adjustments to the busy life swirling around her.

Ninoy, in a way, was also a novice in campaign tactics. But he had a practiced eye and, by watching experienced politicians, quickly learned how the political game worked. Like his opponents, he began to make frequent references to the Bible in his talks. The peasants understood parables and saw their own lives reflected in Bible stories. He also began to talk to his constituents in Pampango.

At age twenty-two, Ninoy won his first election and became the youngest mayor in Philippine history. He would be seated when he reached his twenty-third birthday. Too late he learned that the election may have been illegal, that a candidate had to be twenty-three years old to run for office. Though he took office, he never felt confident of his victory, for the courts would have to decide the legality of the situation.

Now mayor of a small town, a farmer, and a family man, his ambitions were flowering. He gave in to the entreaties of President Magsaysay to become his aide at Malacanang Palace in Manila. Stretching his work day by giving up hours of sleep, he sped daily between Concepcion and Manila. Though the towns are only some sixty-five miles apart, the roads were chopped up and the trip took two hours each way. In the daytime Ninoy was a mayor and farmer. Late afternoon he drove to Malacanang and stayed until dawn. He sat in his palace office going over mail, reading and summarizing the day's news, discussing events with the president, and undertaking special missions. As payment, Ninoy received government funding to build schools, roads, and housing in his community.

The sudden death of President Magsaysay in 1957 in an airplane crash changed the political power structure of the

Malacanang Palace

country. The Philippine Supreme Court, now in different hands, concluded that Ninoy had not been of legal age when he ran for mayor and that he held his office illegally.

Disillusioned and disheartened, Ninoy said good-bye to politics—forever, he thought—and went on to conquer new fields.

He undertook management of Hacienda Luisita in Tarlac, the 17,000-acre sugar plantation recently purchased by Cory's family. It was one of the largest estates in the country, and Ninoy's goal was to update the plantation in every way.

Putting his initiative and energy into the enterprise, he became an expert at farm management. The first problem Ninoy addressed was the discontent of the farm workers. Paternalism had clearly not worked on such a huge plantation, where the tendency was to take advantage of the peasants. Ninoy removed the vestiges of the old-fashioned system and encouraged the farm tenants and laborers to organize into a union with their own labor leaders. He also tried to improve the general living conditions by building better housing, setting up schools and health clinics, and encouraging new skills such as sewing. While these changes were going on, he was converting the plantation into a highly mechanized agri-business by bringing in the most advanced farm technology and experts in farm administration. Within a year, the Hacienda Luisita produced bumper crops and showed huge profits of 40 to 60 percent.

During the years at Luisita, Ninoy again lived alone. Cory had moved to Manila to enter the oldest children in school. The family, in addition to Ballsy, now had another daughter, Aurora Corazon, called Pinky, and a baby son, Benigno III, called Noynoy.

Cory was lonely living without the husband she loved. He was often away, either because of his farm work or he was at political conferences or on government missions. This arrangement, however, was well within the patterns of the times. The husband was the public figure and the woman stayed at home to raise the family. Cory appeared to accept this role and, like her mother before her, was devoted to her children, to whom she transmitted traditional values of religion, discipline, and work.

When necessary, she played a role in Ninoy's resurgent political ambitions. If it meant being a charming hostess to his friends, she served tea or coffee and made small talk, or she helped him during his campaigns.

The country itself could not hold to a steady course. It seemed to seesaw with each president, sometimes strengthening its ties to the United States and at other times signing treaties with eastern countries, in recognition of its Asian roots. Always present was the reality of two U.S. military bases north of Manila. There were repeated scenes of protests by students and nationalist groups, who viewed the bases as symbols of U.S. domination. More objectionable than the bases were the economic entanglements stemming from U.S. investments in the Philippines, such as ownership of plantations and mineral resources. In addition, foreign manufacturers used the islands as a source of cheap labor and, together with favorable tax laws, reaped huge profits. To top the list of problems, foreign bankers dominated the financial market. Though the Philippines had won legal independence in 1946, it became clear to many that the islands were still controlled by the United States.

Contributing to widespread unrest was the corruption that affected even the lowest paid bureaucrat. The country seemed to cry out for an honest leader to take it in hand, to bring about basic change, and steer it onto a course of economic independence and autonomy.

In 1959, Ninoy Aquino was not that person. Though he was an honest man, he was nonetheless vulnerable to scandal because he was identified with the sordid intrigues and payoffs going on in political circles. He had become a strong leader of the Nationalista party and once more entered the race for office. At first he was vice-governor of Tarlac and by 1961 its governor. During this period he held an influential post as secretary of the League of Governors and Mayors. Again he became an aide to the president, this time to Carlos Garcia, who had followed Magsaysay into office. Again he shuttled between Tarlac and Manila to carry out special assignments for the president. Though he was loyal to Garcia, he was aware that government corruption had reached an all-time high, that millions of pesos were mysteriously disappearing from the treasury.

The defeat of Garcia in the 1961 presidential elections also meant the defeat of Ninoy's Nationalista party. A new type of office holder occupied the presidency. Diosdado Macapagal, the candidate of the Liberal party, was committed to wiping out government corruption and its closely connected practice of nepotism, the favors bestowed by officials on relatives. He was also a man of strong national pride. In the hope of defining the country in terms of its own needs and culture, he changed the date of Independence Day from July 4, important in United

States history, to June 12, the day when Aguinaldo announced the first Declaration of Independence at Cavite in 1898. In a step in the same direction, he won an earlier expiration date for the two United States bases. The leases for Subic Bay Naval Base and Clark Air Force Base were now due to expire in 1991.

In 1963, to help stimulate the economy, Macapagal passed the Agrarian Land Reform Code. He also abolished important foreign exchange controls and devalued the peso. But only a handful of people benefited from these changes; most of the Filipino industrialists and workers suffered a setback.

Ninoy, however, as governor of Tarlac province, had to reassess his own position and play the political game. Because he represented the party in opposition to President Macapagal, he was receiving no government funds for local improvements. He wrestled with the idea of switching, of joining the Liberal party as the only way to get funds for his constituency.

In July 1963, Ninoy made the change and took his oath as a Liberal. He called himself "a political turncoat," acknowledging his contempt for such a practice. But support for the president's party resulted in his winning a windfall of funds. He brought so many improvements to the province of Tarlac, in roads, bridges, updated farm machinery, and health clinics, that he was called Santo Ninoy of Tarlac. An added benefit was close ties to Macapagal, with whom he traveled on foreign missions to Cambodia, Indonesia, and North Africa. He was being trained for national office.

# 6

# The Marcos Years

In 1965, a bold, aggressive personality stepped into the leadership of national politics. Ferdinand E. Marcos, a brilliant lawyer-politician, made passionate promises to cleanse the land of its ills.

Born in 1917 in the rural region of Ilocos Norte in northern Luzon, Marcos came from a wealthy and politically active family. Upon his father's election to Congress in 1925, the family moved to Manila.

At an early age Ferdinand Marcos had shown great promise, winning honors throughout his school years. He was blessed with a brilliant mind and an uncanny memory. Educated and accomplished, he presented himself as a military hero in World War II, and in the 1960s, he gripped the nation with his fiery oratory, breathing zeal and promise of change. Twice elected to the house of representatives, he moved on to the senate in 1959.

In 1965, he entered the presidential race on the Nationalista ticket but sounded like a Liberal in campaign speeches. He would fight corruption and crime, he said. He spoke about civil liberties, land reform, and the right of workers to trade union organization.

He easily won the presidential election and ushered in reforms. He made money available for rural areas and for public works such as schools, roads, clinics, and irrigation projects. With the help of United States foundations, and under the expert direction of his staff, new techniques were developed for growing rice. Small acres of land began to yield bumper crops. Called miracle rice, it brought down the price of the staple food, making it more available to the poor.

In foreign policy Marcos strengthened ties to the United States and became the favorite of a succession of presidents there. Lyndon Johnson called him "my right arm in Asia." During the Vietnam War, as in the Korean War, the Philippine government sided with the United States. In 1966, the Marcos government sent the first of a 2,000-member Civic Action Group to South Vietnam. The U.S. bases became fueling and storage depots for the United States air force and navy.

The Marcos support of the U.S. war in Vietnam was not a popular position in the Philippines. Huge student demonstrations took place in front of the United States embassy and at the two bases. These protests were reflections of a growing disenchantment with Marcos and his policies. Land reform turned out to be a failure, leading to increased peasant unrest and rebellion. Equally ineffective for the masses of people were the other reforms. Terming the widespread ferment communist inspired, Marcos sent the military into rural areas to stamp out the agitators. In the search-and-destroy missions, more innocent peasants were killed than rebels. Government violence in the countryside was only one manifestation of growing repression.

To tighten his control over the islands during his early years,

Marcos carefully built a strong political and military apparatus.

The Marcos years were harsh ones for Ninoy Aquino. He was governor of Tarlac and secretary of the League of Governors and Mayors when Marcos was elected president. As a member of the opposition Liberal party, Ninoy had not endorsed Marcos for president, and Marcos would never forget it. At every possible occasion, Marcos singled out Ninoy for attack, often referring to him as a communist or a Huk lover. Violent assaults against Aquino supporters were common and clearly pointed to the actions of Marcos stalwarts. On a local level, government funds for public works in Tarlac dried up, teaching Ninoy again the power of the presidency. The public, aware of the enmity between Marcos and Aquino, saw them as two men squared off in opposite corners, like prizefighters in a ring.

To oppose the tightening military grip over the entire country by the government, and the increased killings and corruption, Ninoy Aquino decided in 1967 to run for senate on the Liberal party ticket. Again he faced the annoying age requirement. He would be nineteen days short of thirty-five, the legal age for a senate seat. He would be thirty-five when he took office, however. Would the courts approve of this?

Ninoy anguished over the situation. But the Marcos machine both inflamed and challenged him. He had to stand up to the corrupt power of the presidency, was the way he saw it. Much to his surprise, Ninoy won the seat, the only candidate on the Liberal party ticket to be victorious. The other candidates swept into office on the Marcos Nationalista party ticket.

Ninoy acknowledged that he could not have won without the help of two important women and their work in Manila. His mother, Dona Aurora, active in the Catholic Women's League, worked on religious organizations and mail campaigns. Always a popular woman, she let everyone know that Ninoy Aquino was her son.

And Cory, now the mother of four with the birth of daughter

Victoria Elisa, called Viel, had become a seasoned campaigner by the time Ninoy ran for senate. Politics and its practical demands had become constant companions from the first year of her marriage. She had always played her role, entertaining friends, serving tea, making small talk. For the senate race, she was actively involved. She visited all the factories in Manila, spoke to hundreds of workers, most of them women. At every marketplace and fiesta, she shook hands and made a prepared little speech: "I am the wife of Ninoy Aquino. I'm sorry he can't be here, so I have come in his behalf." Every day from eight to four, sometimes with eldest daughter Maria Elena along, she campaigned. The child had a small role. "Please vote for my daddy," she would say. Cory also traveled to other regions. On one occasion she flew to Cebu in the south; on another, to La Union in the north, to officiate at the unveiling of a town bell.

Ninoy carefully planned every step of his campaign. To make himself nationally known he was inexhaustible, making do on little sleep and hardly any food. He became a master of small talk. On several occasions he flew around in a helicopter and dropped, as it were, from the heavens. "When you arrive from 2000 feet up, people gather to watch you come down," he said. He shook more hands than he could ever count, and voters in remote barrios would remember the candidate who came to their village to talk to them.

Marcos, violent in his hatred of Ninoy Aquino, continued to refer to him as a friend of the Huks. The name-calling backfired. When the government tried to prevent him from taking his seat because of his age, masses of people, especially students, staged protests demanding that Aquino be seated. To his surprise and jubilation, he won the Supreme Court decision despite every effort by the Marcos government to keep him from office. He was thirty-four, the youngest person to run for the senate, and thirty-five when he took his place in the senate chamber with a battle cry against corruption.

Ninoy no longer owned land in Concepcion, having already

sold his acres to his tenant farmers. The family was finally together in their home on Times Street in Quezon City, on the outskirts of Manila. But Ninoy was a man in perpetual motion. Though he loved his family, he was drawn to outside activities, ones he thought would enhance his national image.

While in the senate he hosted a television program called "Insight." Presented in the form of a travelogue, the show described the countries Senator Aquino had visited, among them Israel, Russia, Taiwan, and Australia. Was he preparing for a higher office? Perhaps the presidency?

In 1969, Marcos easily won reelection, making him the first two-time president of the Philippines. The constitution mandated that this would be his final term. During Marcos's second term, the country was economically on the upswing. Not only the United States but also Japan was a large trading partner. The United States, however, maintained its dominant influence. On the economic side, it was the largest importer of Philippine sugar; and stemming from its control of military, industrial, and financial spheres, it was the second largest employer of Philippine labor.

Though Marcos had been reelected with broad popular backing, scandal in high places weakened his support. His wife, Imelda, was known as a lavish spender, and he himself was accused of personal corruption, of pocketing government monies. Above all, Marcos was accused of nepotism and cronyism, of putting family and close friends in control of profitable industrial and farm enterprises. He was talked about as the richest man in Asia.

Marcos could not control the growing discontent despite his brutal oppression. Crime and corruption were on the increase. In the south, on the island of Mindanao, the Moro people were demanding autonomy; student, peasant, and working-class protest rallies of 20,000 to 50,000 filled the streets with demands for justice.

In late 1968, a new rebel group was organized. Called the

New People's Army (NPA), it is the armed wing of the Philippine Communist party. The group is radical in its approach to change. It said the Philippines were still a semi-feudal, semi-colonial society dominated by the United States. Like other revolutionary movements, NPA members made their homes at first in the mountains and hills of central Luzon. After winning support for its program, the NPA broadened its base and moved freely on many of the islands where it controls farm areas.

Under a different umbrella, the communists formed a coalition called the National Democratic Front (NDF), and drew to their program students, workers, clergy, professionals, and women's groups. Some of these forces joined the insurgents in the hills to become part of the armed revolutionary movement. Marcos's oppression and the beginning deterioration in the economy made it easy for the communists to recruit supporters.

By 1970, when the communists were broadening their base of support, Marcos faced the end of his two-time tenure as president. He called a constitutional convention to rewrite the 1935 constitution gained by the Philippines under commonwealth status. Marcos then pressured convention members to vote for a regulation that would permit a relative to become president. It was public talk that his wife, Imelda, planned to run for office.

In opposition to his plan, a new round of militant demonstrations and rallies took place. Students demonstrated on the Mendiola Bridge, a historic site leading to the palace. Police brutally shot into the crowds, wounding countless demonstrators. The confrontation became known as the Battle of Mendiola.

Police violence did not stop the protests. Students staged a sit-in at the University of the Philippines only to be ruthlessly cleared out by police. Labor strikes, peasant uprisings, and student meetings were all broken up by police and the military.

To make matters worse, the monsoon season brought two storms that destroyed crops in Luzon, swept away bridges and railways, and damaged homes. In the devastation many small businesses and farms were pushed over the edge, contributing to the decline of the economy.

In the face of growing tensions and massive opposition to his government by radicals and centrist democrats, students, workers, and peasants, Marcos at first promised reforms. But he could not contain the crises engulfing the government or the threats to the status quo, in which wealth was concentrated in the hands of a few oligarchs while the masses of people were impoverished. Marcos warned that communists were planning to take over the government. Part of the conspiracy, he said, was Senator Benigno "Ninoy" Aquino.

Ninoy had indeed been a gadfly arousing opposition to Marcos. Though Marcos termed him a communist, Ninoy in no way shared their program for radical change. He hoped to improve conditions within the democratic framework of government. The general talk was that Aquino planned to run for the presidency in the 1973 elections, and that he had a good chance to win the office. He was a highly popular man, and even more so after the magazine *Free Press* named him Man of the Year for 1971 and placed his photo on the cover of one of its issues.

Throughout 1971, explosions and bombs set off in department stores and government buildings gave Marcos the excuse he needed to suspend the writ of habeas corpus, or the right of people not to be imprisoned illegally. Determined to hold on to the presidency, he tightened his grip over the country with the aid of the military and ushered in a new era that would temporarily crush the fighting spirit of the Philippine people.

# 7

# Prison and Exile

On the evening of September 22, 1972, Ninoy Aquino was at a conference at the Hilton Hotel in Manila when police entered the room and arrested him. The arrest had been ordered by Defense Minister Juan Ponce Enrile. That same day and on the following days, thousands of peasant, labor, and student activists were rounded up and hauled off to military compounds.

The day before, September 21, the Marcos government had secretly set up the apparatus for a military state. The police were busy not only arresting activists but padlocking newspaper and magazine offices, closing down television and radio stations, and placing the media under military control.

On September 23, 1972, with all opposition effectively crushed, President Marcos declared a state of martial law. He made his announcement on government-controlled television

A protest march during the Marcos regime is broken up by
water cannons.   PHOTOBANK-PHILIPPINES

and radio stations. Martial law automatically suspended all
civil rights and freedoms. Congress was disbanded, elections
called off, schools closed for a week, and a curfew declared from
midnight to 4 A.M. Everyone owning firearms was ordered to
turn them in.

According to documents recently made public, United States
President Richard Nixon was forewarned of Marcos's intention
and raised no objection to his becoming a dictator.

The legally elected Senator Benigno Aquino, Jr., was, like a
common criminal, whisked away with thousands of others to
a military camp. For most of seven years and seven months, a
small cell at Fort Bonifacio in Makati, Rizal, would be Ninoy's
living quarters. No immediate charges were leveled against the

senator except the general allegation that he had been involved in subversive activities.

At the time of his arrest, Corazon Aquino was at home with their five children, the most recent being year-old Kristine Bernadette. The news of Ninoy's arrest hit her like a physical blow. What did it mean? At first she was numb with fear. Only after many weeks and months would the terror subside.

The first year steeled her. She was now the head of a single-parent household, the mainstay of the family. From the time Ninoy started his political career, she and the family had come second. But he had been on call, available. This was different. For her children she had to show optimism and courage. For Ninoy she was the force that would sustain him during his incarceration, or his captivity, as he called it. He was her beloved and she would do everything possible to help him survive. She would become his public image, a messenger communicating his thoughts to the outside world.

She suffered the worst forty-three days of her life when Ninoy suddenly disappeared. He had been blindfolded and handcuffed and secretly flown from Fort Bonifacio to the dreaded dungeon camp Fort Laur in the province of Nueva Ecija up north. The police had dropped off his clothing, eyeglasses, and watch at the house without saying whether Ninoy was dead or alive. Cory did not know where he was. While she started a search for him, Ninoy was being held in solitary confinement. Because his glasses had been taken away, he suffered blinding headaches. His only clothes were two sets of prison underwear. Fearful that he would be poisoned by drugs added to his food, he only drank water and ate six crackers a day.

For Ninoy Aquino, the nonstop talker, the ebullient, spellbinding orator and dreamer, there was no worse fate than to be forced into solitude and silence. In the suffocating closeness of the four walls of his dark cell, he wrestled with the demons of fear and anguish; he worried over Cory and the family; and he thought of his neglect of them, and his love. In desolation and loneliness he experienced a religious transformation, a transcendent moment, in which his passive religious beliefs changed into profound faith. In a letter to a friend, Ninoy described his tears and suffering, and the fear that he had been forgotten. While he was in the depths of painful self-pity, there came a blinding moment of revelation when he realized that he had, indeed, not been punished but had been blessed with a full life, with talent, and a loving family, that perhaps his present predicament was but a test for a future mission. The realization turned him around and restored his hopes. Strong religious conviction would comfort him for the rest of his life. Not only did he find renewed faith in God but also in the moral belief that the Philippine people were worth fighting for, even dying for. In his prison years Ninoy Aquino made peace with death.

Corazon Aquino, going from office to office and camp to camp to locate Ninoy, was thrown into a strange world. In these surroundings her upper-class privileges offered no protection. She experienced the humbling lot of ordinary people. She joined women who sat for hours outside prison gates waiting to see a son or daughter or husband. She began to identify with those women whose family members had suddenly "disappeared." Like them she was stripped and searched before prison visits. Experienced, however, in the ways of government bureaucracies, she often helped other families of prisoners with their problems.

As Ninoy's surrogate, she was forced out of her home and her private world to become a public figure, to make important decisions. Since her marriage, she had been learning the practical side of politics. Now she had to walk a new track. She was the wife of a political prisoner under a military dictatorship.

During the first year of Ninoy's imprisonment, Cory was strict with the children, forbidding them to go to parties, to shop, or to do anything entertaining. Not until a priest advised her to let go, to let the family lead normal lives, did she loosen her restraints. During that time, too, she had to find a new support network. A few friends and relatives stayed loyal, but many, far too many, turned away from her in church and on the streets. They were afraid to be identified with the "subversive" Senator Aquino and his family.

In April 1973, Ninoy was returned to Fort Bonifacio. In August, he was formally charged by a military tribunal with murder, illegal possession of firearms, and subversion.

Why a military court? Why not a civilian court? he wanted to know. What chance did he have for a fair trial before a military tribunal? Why did the military have jurisdiction over him? He was, after all, a civilian.

He knew he could not get a fair hearing, and he decided to boycott the pretrial proceedings. But before he did so, he delivered a ringing speech denouncing the injustice of the situation. Ending his talk, he said, "Some people suggest that I beg for mercy. But this I cannot in conscience do. I would rather die on my feet with honor, than live on bended knees in shame."

The court audience and newspaper reporters were held spellbound by his emotional outburst. Many realized that he was quoting Dolores Ibarruri, known as La Pasionaria, who had led the Spanish people in the fight against fascism during the Spanish civil war of 1936–1939. In Ninoy's refusal to cringe before the military dictatorship, he won the renewed admiration of the Philippine people.

His case dragged on. By April 1975, he had spent thirty months in jail under maximum security, twenty-four of those months in solitary confinement. To keep his spirits up, he read the works of Mahatma Gandhi and the Reverend Martin Luther King, Jr., the great advocates of nonviolent resistance. He found untapped inner resources in meditation and in writing poetry and letters. For their nineteenth wedding anniversary in 1973, Ninoy wrote a poem for Cory. He called it "I Have Fallen in Love."

> I have fallen in love
> With the same woman three times
> In a day spanning nineteen years
> Of tearful joys and joyful tears.
> . . . . . . . . . . . . . . . . .
> My only escape is to cling
>     to the woman of my dreams
> Who gave me a life full of love,
>     a love full of life,
> She is my urge to live,
>     my sole motivation to survive,
> She taught me not only to dream,
>     but to make dreams alive.
> Fight on! she says. . . .

In another poem he called Cory an "impregnable rock
. . . the memory that haunts me to the deepest cave."

Though she appeared self-contained, Cory nevertheless de-
spaired over Ninoy's uncertain fate. In front of him she remained quiet, resolute, secretly smuggling his writings and
letters out of prison. She developed an underground press for
distribution of his writings to friends.

When the Aquino case was finally called before the military
tribunal in April 1975, Ninoy refused to participate in the trial,
calling it an unconscionable mockery. The court nevertheless
forced him to be present at the proceedings. To publicize the
gross injustice of the situation, Ninoy went on a hunger strike.
He said his action was one of protest not only for himself but
"for the many thousands of Filipinos who are helpless victims
of the oppression and injustices of the so-called New Society."
A man, he said, "must prefer a meaningful death to a meaning-
less life."

It was Cory's job to publicize his act. She called a news
conference at their Times Street home. Through the media the

Corazon Aquino speaks at a political rally.   T. ROCAMORA /
PHILIPPINE INFORMATION OFFICE, SAN FRANCISCO

country learned of Ninoy's determination to expose the fraud
of the military dictatorship.

At the end of a forty-day hunger strike, Ninoy had become
a pale, frail figure. He entered court leaning on someone's arm.
Friends were shaken by his appearance. His suffering was so
intense that life after the hunger strike was a bonus, he said. But
the starvation and tension had weakened his heart.

Finally, after two years of anguished waiting, the Aquino
family and friends were in court when the military tribunal

handed down its decision in November 1977. Ninoy Aquino
was sentenced to death by a firing squad. The verdict shocked
the country. Ninoy himself suffered a heart attack and was
rushed to a hospital.

Worldwide public pressure forced Marcos to rescind the
order of execution. But Ninoy remained in jail.

Over the years of imprisonment and detention, Ninoy had
gained a few privileges. Among them were weekend conjugal
visits. From 10 A.M. Saturday to 1 P.M. Sunday, Cory had
Ninoy to herself. Her joy at being "alone" with Ninoy in his cell
was not destroyed, though she knew that every moment was
monitored by an electric eye and listening devices. For Cory
Aquino these were special hours that she would never forget,
hours of closeness when they could exchange private thoughts
and she could give him reports on the week's events. A special
dispensation from the minister of defense made it possible for
the children to visit their father in his cell and stay overnight.
Ninoy spoke to them freely about his suffering and his political
hopes.

While all opposition voices were silenced and the people
intimidated, Marcos instituted his grand plan to revamp the
country. He called it the New Society. Central to his ideas was
a strong military, without whom, Marcos claimed, he could not
carry out his goal to improve the country's economy and pro-
ductivity. To expand the military's role in government, he increased the military budget from 800 million pesos to 4 billion.
At the same time, military leaders were given new privileges as
well as new responsibilities. They were in control of the trade-
union movement, the press, youth, mass organizations, and
many aspects of civilian life.

Though the New Society promised land reform, the proce-
dures to effect land changes remained centrally, not locally
controlled and were therefore ineffective. Instead, the owner-

ship of farming by large corporate organizations was on the increase. Industry was oriented more to the export market than to domestic needs.

During the years of his military dictatorship, Marcos had the support of the United States government. He extended to U.S. industrialists preferential terms for economic investments. Moreover, he made the United States' jurisdiction over its two bases clear and safe. In return for favors, the United States increased its military and economic assistance to the Marcos government.

In 1978, Marcos, forced to loosen his military hold, called for the election of an interim National Assembly, a legislative body with limited power. Before the election, he formed the New Society Movement (KBL), a political organization to support his candidates for the assembly.

From his jail cell, Ninoy Aquino announced his intention to run for an assembly seat on the Laban, or People's party, ticket. He became the focus of the Marcos opposition in Manila and other large cities.

Cory Aquino, in becoming his campaign manager, emerged fully into political life. She held news conferences, arranged for committees of volunteers, and spread his message through leaflets and posters. To encourage him, she arranged for a "noise barrage" outside his cell window so he could hear the shouting, whistling, and clamor of his supporters. The children also campaigned for their father, especially Ballsy, the oldest; his son, Noynoy; and seven-year-old Kris. The government even permitted the former senator to make a brief television appearance.

Ninoy lost the election, as did everyone on the opposition ticket. Only Marcos loyalists gained office. Among them was Imelda Marcos, who had "won" a seat in the assembly and who became a powerful political figure in her own right.

Under eased detention regulations, Ninoy was permitted a

President Marcos and First Lady Imelda Marcos cut the ribbon during the opening ceremony for the first Manila Film Festival, January 18, 1979. PHILIPPINE INFORMATION OFFICE

home visit in 1979 to celebrate his and Cory's twenty-fifth wedding anniversary. On Christmas he was again permitted home.

In March 1980, Ninoy suffered a second heart attack, far more severe than the first. Medical diagnosis revealed he had a life-threatening condition that required immediate surgery. While in the hospital, he had an unexpected visit from Imelda Marcos. The two spent an hour and a half together, at the end of which Ninoy was given permission to leave for the United States for a heart bypass operation. There was an understanding that he would remain in the United States, an exile.

Cory and three of the children—two remained in school—traveled with Ninoy to the Baylor Medical Center in Dallas, Texas. After his successful heart surgery and convalescence, the family moved to the Boston area and found a home in Newton, Massachusetts.

Though the New Society Movement held out the promise of restoring the Philippines to democracy, it succeeded only in further entrenching itself by putting into office Marcos's relatives and friends. Imelda Marcos had become governor of Metro Manila and minister of human settlements.

By 1981, under growing domestic and foreign pressure, the Marcos government lifted martial law. Later that year, it put into effect the 1973 constitution, which placed no limits on the number of presidential terms. Marcos was reelected for another six years. In practice the presidency remained a military dictatorship and Ferdinand Marcos the absolute ruler.

# 8 | Death at a Manila Airport

The Aquinos settled into a red brick, Georgian-style house on Commonwealth Avenue in Newton, Massachusetts. Cory would refer to the three years in the spacious house in Chestnut Hill, as the area was called, as the happiest of her life. She spent private time with Ninoy and watched the family patch up relationships. They also bought a country home in nearby Brookfield. Many weekends were spent in the rural quiet of an old colonial house set on sixteen acres of land overlooking a lake.

In those peaceful years Kris, the youngest, got to know her father. She had been only a year old when he was put in prison. Now she enjoyed the give-and-take between them. She often watched news broadcasts with him when she returned from the nearby Catholic school she attended. Though she did not always share his point of view, she nevertheless enjoyed their lively discussions.

Cory once again stepped back into a quiet private life. Neighbors in Newton reported only rare glimpses of her, though they often saw Ninoy along the streets walking the family dog or doing one chore or another. To Cory, Ninoy was the boss. She would jestingly refer to him as a male chauvinist, though she seemed to accept her role in the family. She had been in the public eye for seven years during Ninoy's imprisonment, handling complex matters. Now once again journalists described her as a woman "who served refreshments and remained in the background at Commonwealth Avenue."

It must have seemed to Cory Aquino that she was serving refreshments day and night, for their home was always crowded with people. Friends, admirers, and relatives came to visit and stayed for days. Ninoy's birthdays, in particular, became gala events celebrated by as many as one hundred people. Among them were colleagues from both Harvard University and the Massachusetts Institute of Technology, where Ninoy had become a research fellow and guest lecturer.

Ninoy would say that his two years at Harvard's Center for International Affairs were like a dream come true. In talks with scholars he developed his own intellectual capacity.

Above all, Ninoy was the center for the exiled Filipino community and a leader of his political party, Laban. In long, endless meetings, he discussed with his confreres the worsening conditions in the Philippines and how they could end the Marcos dictatorship.

The former senator Ninoy Aquino was on top of every statistic. He could tick off figures and details of the economy the way others could count from one to ten.

He discussed the increasing poverty and the daily hunger of the farm population. In both cities and countryside, children scavenged in garbage heaps for food. The enormous wealth of his country, he knew, was no longer spread out among the elite class but was now concentrated in the hands of the Marcos family and a few cronies. They dipped into the government

Crowded shanties in Manila   UN PHOTO

treasury as if it were a private bank account, making millions
of dollars available for their personal use. Their extravagant
self-indulgence and corruption had become worldwide scan-
dals.

He was well informed about the economic advantages arranged for foreign manufacturers. Most of them owned factories on Bataan in a fenced-off enclave called the Bataan Export
Processing Zone. In 1981, there were fifty-eight enterprises
within the enclave, employing thousands of workers, 90 percent
of whom were women. They had become a source of cheap
labor, working long hours at low pay.

He read reports of the Philippine human rights organizations
and church groups and knew that people were accused of sub-

Women laborers in foreign-owned factory in Bataan Export
Processing Zone   THIRD WORLD REPORTS

version because they protested their living conditions; that they
were thrown into jail, tortured, and killed; that children were
often victims of police brutality and torture.

He followed the uprisings of the Muslims in their age-old
quest for independence and he watched with alarm the growing
strength of the armed revolutionary force, the New People's
Army. They had spread out from Luzon to become a nationwide movement, in some areas controlling 20 percent of the
countryside. They had some 15,000 to 20,000 people under
arms. Not only the poor but the middle class were joining
their movement. Nuns and priests, in order to help the poor,
fled to the hills to work with the NPA. They had nothing to
lose, the new recruits said, in joining the fight for land reform,

universal education, and health and social programs. The youth, too, were flocking to the hills to take up arms in the struggle.

To seek solutions to his country's problems, Ninoy met with emissaries from other third world nations. He traveled to Nicaragua, Lebanon, and some African countries to see how these governments were handling their problems. He was convinced that the only path for the Philippines was in a democratic, nonviolent revolution.

Though surrounded by loving family and friends, he was nevertheless an exile. And he was getting restless. He could not quiet the voice within him, a growing dream, that he could bring sanity to his country.

He talked of returning home. He belonged among his people, he said.

In the spring of 1983 he said the time had come. He had learned through the grapevine of President Marcos's deteriorating health. Political talk was that his wife, Imelda Marcos, would become the next president. If not Imelda, then the military would take over the government.

By May 1983, Ninoy's decision was definite. He was going to return to the Philippines and run in the elections for National Assembly scheduled for May 1984.

What did Ninoy Aquino hope to accomplish by his return? He spoke of his dreams and hopes in an interview he gave a journalist in Boston on August 1, 1983, two weeks before his departure.

His main goal was to have a personal talk with President Marcos. He wanted one single hour with him, that was all. In that hour he would plead with the president to restore full democratic rights and freedoms to the country. This, according to Ninoy, could be brought about through the process of "national unity and reconciliation." For that hour he was willing to risk his life.

In the event Marcos refused to see him, Ninoy would lead the people in mass nonviolent demonstrations.

Clearly outlined in his mind was a program to put the country on its feet. He spoke to the interviewer about "mass employment rather than corporate profit." He spoke about land reform, and freedom for workers to have collective bargaining and to strike. He said he thought the two U.S. bases would have to be phased out. And he pointed to a dangerous situation in which the Philippines were losing their independence through huge debts to foreign banks.

Ninoy knew the possible fate that awaited him—a death sentence, or prison once again. He brushed aside the pleas of friends, colleagues, his spiritual adviser, and his mother—all urging him not to return.

Cory learned of death threats, that Ninoy would be killed if he set foot in the Philippines. She feared for his safety and at the same time thought it useless for him to embark on his mission, that he would not succeed. But she knew Ninoy thoroughly, that he was a man of dreams and ambition. To engage him in continuous arguments was futile.

Another person urged him not to return. Imelda Marcos, on a trip to New York, met with Ninoy and told him to remain in the United States where he had a good life with his family. She explained that the Philippine government would provide him with security if he returned but still could not guarantee his safety.

Despite all the pleading, Ninoy could not be dissuaded. On Saturday, August 13, he took a flight from Boston to Los Angeles, California. After a few days there, he took a connecting flight to Taipei, the capital of Taiwan, where he landed on Friday, August 19. Met there by his brother-in-law, a newspaper reporter, he was again warned of death threats, that plans had been made for his assassination.

While in Taipei, Ninoy spoke to Cory by phone. To comfort

him, she read him passages from the Bible. He spoke to each of the children. Journalists traveling with him reported that he broke down in tears after the phone talks. He took the time to write each of his children a letter.

On August 21, 1983, Ninoy boarded a plane for Manila International Airport, where 20,000 supporters and friends had gathered to greet him. They waved yellow banners; their buses and jeeps were draped in yellow. The air was filled with the voices of thousands singing a favorite song, "Tie a Yellow Ribbon Round the Old Oak Tree." This popular American song tells about a prisoner who returns to his hometown after a long absence and finds that his lady love has tied a yellow ribbon around an old tree, a sign that she still loves him. Yellow had become a symbol of love and support.

Ninoy wore a bullet-proof jacket and, under it, a rosary. Three security guards were assigned to protect him.

He had prepared a statement to read to his welcomers, was about to step from the plane, when he was unexpectedly whisked to a side exit by armed soldiers, out of sight of his supporters. He walked down the nineteen narrow steps to the tarmac. A volley of shots rang out, hitting Ninoy in the head. He died instantly, spread out on the tarmac at Manila International Airport while his friends waited to greet him.

Corazon Aquino's personal grief was buried under the shock and horror of the assassination. Dutifully she stepped before the television cameras and media people who crowded into her Chestnut Hill living room. According to one report, she sobbed briefly, "I didn't think it would come to this." Then she became a grief-stricken woman who showed the public a face under control.

A week later she and the family returned to the Philippines. At once Corazon Aquino was swept up in the emotional outpourings of millions. "You are not alone," they said to her in banners, flowers, and other messages of support. For ten days, lines of people filed past Ninoy's coffin.

Public outpouring of grief and rage directed against Marcos
JOHN CHUA

Around the world the public reacted with stunned disbelief. Within the Philippines the cruel assassination unleashed massive demonstrations of rage. Shock, grief, and loss overwhelmed the people, changing them, making them radical in opposition to the Marcos government, whom they blamed for the murder. Thousands who had never acted politically filled the streets, marched, and shouted their anger in front of Malacanang Palace.

In the funeral cortege, the largest in Philippine history, it was estimated that two million mourners walked through the streets behind the black-clad figure of Corazon Aquino and the flower-filled bier. It took eleven hours for the procession to cover the eighteen miles from the church in Quezon City to Manila Memorial Park where Benigno Aquino, Jr., was buried.

Ninoy's funeral cortege  JOHN CHUA

In her message broadcast over the Catholic radio station,
Cory Aquino demanded justice, not only for her slain husband
but for all others unjustly killed; she asked for restoration of
freedom for a suffering nation under bondage. In resounding
words she vowed to continue her husband's opposition to President Marcos: He will not have died in vain, she said.

Though Cory Aquino may have wanted to retire to the privacy of her grief, she was not permitted to do so. In the public
demand to see her and hear her, she became the continuing
symbol of her husband's fight for freedom. She would say during election campaigns, "When I saw [my husband] in his
coffin, with his bloodstained shirt, I promised him I would
continue the struggle for justice." Ninoy Aquino had become
a martyr in the fight for democratic rights, and the Philippine

people demanded that Corazon Aquino carry that struggle forward.

Three months after the assassination, Cory Aquino returned to the United States for a memorial service to Benigno S. Aquino, Jr., at St. Paul's church in Harvard Square, Cambridge. People commented that she had changed, that she seemed more confident. All agreed that she was completely in command of the situation.

# 9

# A Public Figure

From the moment of Ninoy Aquino's assassination, Corazon Aquino became an acclaimed public figure. The shy woman learned to address huge rallies. There was so much rage in her, it did not seem difficult to speak her mind before thousands of people and to become the gadfly her husband had been. She prodded people into action against the Marcos government, to demand an honest investigation into her husband's murder.

Not the orator her husband had been, she was nevertheless magnetic. Perhaps it was her simplicity and straightforward manner, perhaps her modest dress. Usually earrings were her only ornament. She wore eyeglasses and had her thick dark hair short cropped. Her figure was lithe, giving ease and grace to her movements. Speaking from a stage or hastily erected platform, she would flash a luminous smile in greeting and then, in a lilting voice, deliver her message, urging people forward to talk out against Marcos, to demand his resignation. Her presence itself was a reminder that something ugly was going on in high places, and that she was taking on the role that had belonged to her husband.

Commemorations of Ninoy's death and birthday turned into huge rallies. Tens of thousands came to hear Cory Aquino talk on September 21, 1983, one month after Ninoy's murder. Called the National Day of Sorrow, the event was called to mourn not only Ninoy's death but also the end of democratic government ten years before. After the meeting, 15,000 people marched to Malacanang Palace by way of the Mendiola Bridge. They were stopped by a phalanx of police and marines, who shot into the crowd, killing eleven people and wounding hundreds. Another brutal episode was added to the country's history.

After the confrontation, military police fortified Malacanang Palace by stringing wire across the bridge to keep protesters away. Despite the fact that the palace grounds had been turned into a fortress, protests, rallies, and vigils continued to take place on the bridge in the escalating demand to end the Marcos dictatorship.

Corazon Aquino had rejected the government explanation of her husband's murder as the act of one crazed individual. Her insistence, and the insistence of thousands of others, forced the Marcos government to form a special commission to investigate the death. In the ensuing months, the five-member citizens' panel concluded that the murder had been planned and executed by the country's highest ranking military, including Marcos's chief of staff, General Fabian Ver. After a ten-month trial, all were acquitted by the Marcos-appointed tribunal.

Cory Aquino would never be satisfied with the court decision, and she hoped someday to bring these same men to trial under a democratic government, when the sentence might fit the crime.

Ninoy's assassination brought about a resurgence of political activism, especially on the part of women. Working women and wealthy women marched through the business districts wearing WE LOVE NINOY T-shirts. They carried banners demanding IMELDA RESIGN! and handed out leaflets explaining that they were "tired of lies, injustice, and economic crises."

Among the many organizations that sprang up in late 1983 and 1984 was a coalition of women's groups called GA-BRIELA. In a militant program they made known the punishing effects of the declining economy on women and children, and they called attention to the many women who had been tortured and killed in Marcos's jails.

All the grass-roots organizations were united in their opposition to the Marcos government. The problem was to maintain that unity—and it was threatened—as the May 1984 elections approached.

Laban, Ninoy's party, was divided on the question of whether to support or boycott the elections. Opponents claimed that the elections would not be honest and that Marcos would have the final say no matter who won. At times debate was so bitter that family members were divided against one another. Though Cory listened to both sides of the argument, she could not at first resolve her own conflict.

After much soul-searching, she came out for participation and explained her reasons in a nationwide address over the Catholic church's radio station. In an emotional speech she recalled that Ninoy had planned to run for office in the May elections. Like him, she said, she was "committed to the restoration of democracy through peaceful means." She called on President Marcos to avert violence and to guarantee safe elections for the participation in the electoral process by "as broad a spectrum of Philippine society as possible."

In the ensuing months, meetings, rallies, and marches further split the Marcos opposition. In a march from the southern islands through the country up to Manila, thousands called for a boycott. Though this position was endorsed by many mem-

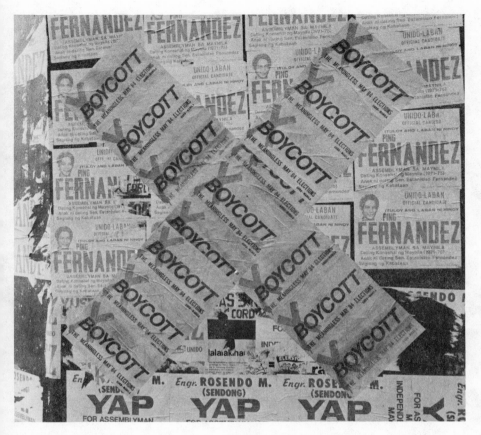

Posters urge citizens to boycott the May 1984 elections. THE
GUARDIAN

bers of trade unions and the radical movements, it also had a
fair degree of support among moderates. Nasty remarks directed at Cory claimed that she had betrayed her husband's
ideals. She was adamant in her position, however, and urged the
Philippine people to go to the polls.

She had become a popular speaker, drawing huge crowds in
campaign speeches across the archipelago. She made a special
appeal to the young who had grown up under Marcos and never
gone to the polls. You must challenge Marcos, she said, and the
only way to do so is in the voting booth.

Anti-Marcos sentiment was worldwide. This demonstration took place in New York City.   TONY YARUS/THE GUARDIAN

The Catholic church supported participation and, through the watchdog committee, NAMFREL, sent 10,000 volunteers into the countryside to oversee the voting. The usual fraud took place, while poll watchers documented the long list of irregularities. They mentioned an incomplete list of candidates, the stuffing of ballot boxes, intimidation by soldiers and police, and violence by armed thugs.

When 80 percent of the people turned out to vote, sending fifty-six opposition candidates to office, Corazon Aquino had won the day. In a victory speech she gave credit to people power, to popular determination to struggle against corruption through democratic means. Cory Aquino had been beloved as Ninoy's widow, but now she developed into a hero in her own right. In the consensus of national politics, she emerged as a leading figure, one who could unite the opposition to Marcos. Her skills, she knew, had not sprung forth at once full-blown. She had been nurtured by the best teacher in politics, she would say, and she meant Ninoy Aquino.

Though she was known to yearn for the privacy of home and family, that wish receded. The Philippine people had found in her a treasure, a firm, unafraid, magnetic personality whose very presence inspired them to lift their voices.

Not only was she a national figure, but she had captured worldwide admiration. Cory watchers were learning through television and other media how this woman was taking on the reins of authority and dealing with the needs of her country.

She continued to capture news headlines when, soon after the May elections, she visited the United States. Among the honors bestowed on her that spring was one she particularly enjoyed. Her alma mater, the College of Mount Saint Vincent, gave her an honorary degree of Doctor of Humane Letters. In her acceptance speech, she spoke about courage, which she called "a spiritual staying-power which enables a person to die for the one he or she loves. It is a quality which transcends fear."

The change in Corazon Aquino from shy student to public speaker of poise and charm was noted by college friends and teachers. Though still quiet and self-contained, she now radiated self-confidence.

Continuing her political leadership, in December 1984, she joined two others, one a businessman and the other a former senator, to form the Convenor group. Its purpose was to devise a system to select a single opposition candidate in the event Marcos called a snap, or immediate, presidential election. She let it be known that she herself had no political ambitions, though she clearly wished to have a voice in decision making.

Despite her protests, she was viewed as the most charismatic figure in the country, a woman who had tested her skills and popularity in battle.

New political groupings quickly formed. Early 1985 saw the organization of Bayan, the New Patriotic Alliance, made up primarily of factions within the ruling elite. Her brother-in-law, Agapito Aquino, helped put together the August 21 movement called ATOM, asking for the withdrawal of the two U.S. bases. In October 1985, a movement was launched to draft Cory Aquino for president.

Before she committed herself as a presidential candidate, Cory Aquino raised two conditions, hoping they would not be met. She agreed to run for office if Marcos would announce a snap election and also if she received petitions with one million signatures endorsing her candidacy.

One month later, Marcos, pressured by the opposition and the United States, announced presidential elections for early 1986. He had deliberately given short notice, hoping to keep the opposition in disarray. And Cory was presented with more than a million signatures.

Both conditions now fulfilled, Corazon Aquino filed the proper papers for candidacy for president of the Philippines. Her running mate for vice-president would be Salvador Laurel, an old-time liberal. By mid-December 1985, a rally of tens of thousands proclaimed Aquino and Laurel candidates of UNIDO, the leading opposition party.

More than anyone, Cory Aquino knew the hard work, planning, meetings, and campaigning required. Like Ninoy, she was now away from home and the family for sixteen hours a day.

She campaigned like a trouper, answering nasty remarks with simple retorts. To the comment that she had no experience, she replied, "It is true I have no experience in lying, cheating, stealing, and killing. I offer you honesty and sincerity

Philippine police protect the U.S. embassy, 1985. THIRD
WORLD REPORTS

in leadership." To others she promised, if elected, "not to live
in Malacanang. I will open it up to the people."

She spoke before women, peasants, workers, and students as
well as upper-class civic groups. To them all, she was a symbol
of an uncorrupted woman, a woman they could trust.

She made no great promises about immediately solving the
staggering problems of the bankrupt country. It seemed
enough, at the moment, to topple a brutal dictatorship, to
restore civil rights and liberties, to open up "democratic space,"
as she called it. Only with patience, and through "peace and
reconciliation," would the country be able to move forward.

Her popularity reached a high point when one million people
showed up at a post-election rally in Luneta Park in Manila on
February 16. On February 25, Corazon Aquino was sworn in
as the seventh president of the Philippines in a political upset
that has been called historic.

# 10

# The Voice of Corazon Aquino

Throughout the first few months in office, President Aquino took steps to restore civil rights within a democratic structure. It meant dismantling the Marcos apparatus of government, removing his appointees from office, and in many cases retiring his generals.

Before she took office, the president let it be known that she would keep her promise not to move into Malacanang Palace, the historic home of government officials. The palace represented to her the corruption and cruelty of the Marcos regime, and she did not wish to be identified with its abuses. Instead, she converted the palace into a museum so the public could view for itself the wasteful extravagance of the Marcos family. A small guest house on the palace grounds became her office. Into another guest house she moved her family from their large home in Quezon City.

President Aquino stands with her son Noynoy, *at right,* and her daughters, sons-in-law, and grandchild in their home on the palace grounds. MEDIA OFFICE, MANILA

Along with the president's faith in democracy is her profound religious faith, a mystique that surrounds her as a person and politician. Frequently prayer power and people power become interchangeable. She is supported by the traditional wing of the Catholic church in a country that is 80 percent Catholic. Her faith is a form of bonding with the people. She also plays a special role for women, who hope she will listen to them and respond to their particular needs.

President Aquino moved swiftly to take on responsibilities and, on her second day in office, formed her cabinet. She also created the Presidential Commission on Good Government. This group was empowered to search for and reclaim the billions of dollars stolen by the Marcos government and hidden away in foreign real estate and secret bank accounts.

Intent on upholding civil and human rights, she reestablished the writ of habeas corpus suspended by Marcos in 1971. Once again people were given protection against illegal imprisonment. She removed restraints on freedom of the press and on the rights of labor.

Fulfilling a campaign promise, she announced the unconditional release from jail of some five hundred political prisoners, including communists, an act that drew both applause and criticism.

By mid-March, the president created the Committee on Human Rights, abolished the old National Assembly filled with Marcos followers, and adopted a provisional Freedom Constitution.

The opening up of democratic space was not only to benefit the people but necessary for the president herself. She is deeply committed to the democratic process, for through freedom of expression she can hear a broad range of popular opinion. Perhaps these voices will help her enact bold programs to meet the staggering problems she inherited on coming into office. She had already established a pattern of listening to all sides of a question and then finding a middle course. She also has confidence in her own intelligence and skills, in her ability to grasp details. She often asks for time, that people have patience. But some problems are critical and time may not be available.

One of the gravest conditions facing the new president is the poverty within the country. The previous government had tightened wealth in the hands of a few, while 70 percent of the present population of 56 million live below the poverty line. Unemployment stands at an all-time high of 25 percent. Behind the statistics are human beings: people suffering the violence of famine—thin, spindly children dying of hunger; women and men scarred by malnutrition and despair.

The poverty is visible everywhere. In Manila 25,000 people

Young boy scavenges through garbage.   ROBERT GUMPERT/
THE GUARDIAN

live clumped together into the space of a fifth of a mile, without
sanitation facilities and with only communal faucets and occa-
sional electricity. They search through garbage dumps for food
and clothing.

Facts hidden by the Marcos government are emerging from
the island of Negros, where unemployment skyrocketed from
falling sugar prices. Families were forced out of decent housing
into dusty, ramshackle shanties to suffer the painful fate of the
hungry in high death tolls and disease.

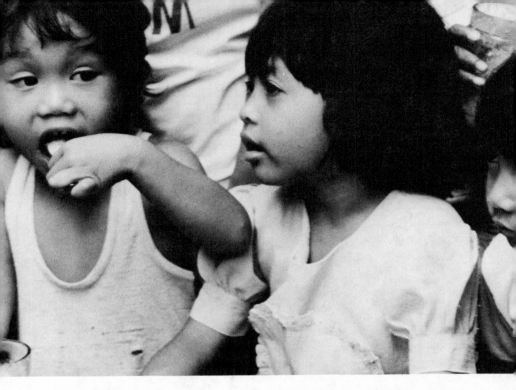

Children on the island of Negros   JOHN SILVA, OXFAM AMER-
ICA

The starving find it difficult to obey the president's request
for patience or to understand her statement, "Believe me when
I say that my government is out eventually to redress your
grievances."

Why can't the president enact a solid program for famine
relief?

The answer is partially found in the interrelated problems of
a bankrupt treasury and a huge foreign debt of 27 billion dollars. President Aquino is not the head of a superpower or a
heavily industrialized country. The Philippines belong to the
third world group of nations, those that are undeveloped or
underdeveloped. As in many such countries, the economy rests
on investments by foreign corporations. These investors de-
velop industry and agriculture for export rather than for the
country's own needs. For example, clothing is manufactured to

be shipped abroad, and huge plantations grow pineapples and coconuts for export when the people need food crops.

The Philippines are heavily in debt to foreign banks and the International Monetary Fund (IMF). In many ways these creditors control the domestic policies the president can adopt. They want money directed first and foremost toward the repayment of loans. If this is not done, they threaten to cut off future loans and investments. It becomes a dizzying spiral of which comes first: feeding the poor or repaying the foreign debt.

Saddling the Aquino government is another debt—the expenses incurred in building the Bataan Nuclear Power Plant across Manila Bay. Constructed by the Marcos government to bring energy to the Philippines when the price of oil went sky-high, the lease was given to the U.S. firm Westinghouse. It constructed the plant at a cost of over 2.1 billion dollars, some of which found its way into the private bank accounts of government officials. In addition, new sources reveal that Westinghouse paid Marcos and an associate a bribe of 25 to 40 million dollars to win the contract. The Aquino government is obligated to pay a huge yearly interest though it has vowed never to operate the plant, which was built on the site of an earthquake fault and only six miles from an active volcano.

High on the list of difficult problems is the one concerning the U.S.–controlled naval and air force bases in the Philippines. Clark Air Force Base and Subic Bay Naval Base are the two largest overseas installations. Strategically located on the island of Luzon north of Manila, they are considered by the United States to be vital to its global military strategy and Asian policy. From those bases the United States can move easily into connecting sea lanes to monitor events on the Asian mainland and in the entire Far East.

The bases have a U.S. staff of 16,000, plus 9,000 or so sailors who come off visiting U.S. naval vessels; in addition they employ a Filipino work force of 40,000.

The bases have been a source of conflict from the first days

Two aspects of the U.S. presence in the Philippines—*above,*
demonstrators for a nuclear-free nation   KAREN VANDER
PLOEG/UNITED CHURCH BOARD FOR WORLD MINISTRIES;
*below,* the front gate of Clark Air Force Base   THIRD WORLD
REPORTS

of installation, irksome to the national pride of a people who resent these symbols of foreign domination. A broad anti-base coalition of many organizations demands the dismantling of all foreign bases in Asia to achieve a non-nuclear, self-determined Asia and Pacific.

President Aquino is caught in the predicament of requiring economic aid from the United States, yet she has refused, so far, to extend the lease on the bases, which expires in 1991. She expects the Philippine people to make that decision.

While faced with these acute problems, she is hampered by the lack of unity within the country. Though she is commander-in-chief of the armed services, she has been besieged by repeated attempts at military coups to overthrow her government. The army shelters not only Marcos loyalists but also troops loyal to Juan Ponce Enrile, who is known to have presidential ambitions. Because of Enrile's divisiveness, President Aquino has forced him to resign from the cabinet. Both Marcos and Enrile represent conservative interests who are demanding increased military measures against the communist insurgency. The military continues to foment trouble by its violent actions, which include setting off bombs in public places, killing innocent peasants, and threatening social activists.

Though of a different nature, the New People's Army is also a threat to the government, because of its militant tactics and demands for radical change. The disfranchised, the hungry, and the homeless become the recruits to the communist insurgency. While hoping not to use military force against the insurgents, President Aquino nevertheless faces great pressure to do just that. She has repeated time after time that the Marcos government tried for seventeen years to wipe out the rebels militarily only to have them grow from a force of a few hundred into many thousands.

Though President Aquino tries to disregard the threats from the right and left, foreign investors see the Philippines as unstable for new economic ventures.

Angry citizens object to U.S. military aid to their country.
PHOTOBANK-PHILIPPINES

To work out solutions to some of these problems and to establish herself in the council of nations, President Aquino undertook trips abroad. In August 1986, she visited Indonesia and Singapore. In September, she accepted an invitation from President Ronald Reagan to visit the United States. She hoped to establish new financial connections; urge foreign investments; reschedule debt payments; get new loans; and, above all, obtain immediate economic aid. On the lighter side she planned to meet with members of the large Philippine–United States community who had been active on her behalf and to visit old friends.

Wherever she traveled on her U.S. visit, President Aquino was honored and feted. At all her speaking engagements, she was greeted by supporters and familiar symbols of affection: yellow balloons, yellow flowers and pins, yellow leaflets and posters.

President Aquino arrives in San Francisco. T. ROCAMORA/
PHILIPPINE INFORMATION OFFICE, SAN FRANCISCO

In her former hometown of Newton, Massachusetts, she
found that the house on Commonwealth Avenue had been
converted into the Benigno S. Aquino Memorial Foundation.

At Harvard University she spoke emotionally, recalling
Ninoy Aquino's happy years there. She described his commitment to nonviolent action, a commitment that is now hers. She
described the women in her campaign, especially those who had
tied themselves to ballot boxes to protect them from Marcos
officials. "My political strength," she told the audience, "rests
on popular support . . . in people power and the nonviolent
approach."

She continued to win admirers, especially when she addressed both houses of the United States Congress. She was
outspoken in her need for economic aid. Equally frank was her
assessment of the communist insurgency, which many in Congress wanted her to crush at once by military means. That was

not the answer, she insisted. Marcos went at it that way, "with hammer and tongs," she said. "By the time he fled, that insurgency had grown to more than 16,000. I think there is a lesson here to be learned about trying to stifle a thing with the means by which it grows." She said the answer to the insurgency was to remove the causes which help it grow, and that meant bringing about economic progress and justice within the country.

In her impassioned statements, she explained to the members of Congress that she "must explore the path of peace to the utmost." Should that path fail, then she would "consider laying down the olive branch of peace and taking up the sword of war."

On this visit her old college, Mount Saint Vincent, again claimed her, bestowing on her its highest honor, the Elizabeth Seton medal.

Every stop on her visit received wide media coverage. She was described in newspapers, captured on television screens, and written up in magazines as if she were a film idol. By being herself, she was elegant. Her intelligence and wit were sparkling, showing her poised in every situation and in control of the material she was delivering. This was clearly the case in her talk on September 22 to the delegates of the world's powers at the United Nations, where she was an honored guest.

She startled the delegates with her bold comments, rebuking them for not supporting the people of her country against a military dictatorship. She reminded them that one year before, Imelda Marcos addressed them. She spoke out to the oppressed people of the world, telling them that they must by themselves implement the ideals for which the United Nations stands, that through their struggles they could bring about human rights and freedom from oppression.

She reached out to Nelson and Winnie Mandela, the embattled leaders of the African National Congress. This militant organization has been fighting against South Africa's brutal racist system called apartheid. For his leadership Nelson Man-

President Aquino, *above,* speaking to America's National Women's Political Caucus in Washington, D.C. JAMES K. GRIMES; and, *below,* addressing the UN General Assembly, September 22, 1986 UN PHOTO

dela has been in jail for twenty-two years. His wife, Winnie Mandela, has been in and out of prison many times. "My prayers are with you," President Aquino said. "Mr. Mandela's long incarceration in prison, separated from his wife and family, inevitably reminds me of the imprisonment of my own husband, Ninoy Aquino." She then announced that her country would "support any action of the international community to hasten . . . peace and freedom in South Africa and to show solidarity with its people."

By October President Aquino had returned home buoyed with renewed confidence in her abilities. She had won a reluctant promise of immediate economic aid from the United States. And she had made it abundantly clear that foreign banks must loosen the strangling effect of debt repayments, that unless they did so a fragile democracy could not survive.

She turned her attention at once to gain endorsement for the constitution she was presenting to the country for a referendum on February 2, 1987. The vote would be a test of her popular support. Opposition to the constitution came from both extreme right and extreme left. The conservative forces did not want to see the Aquino presidency legalized. The radical left found the new constitution weak in measures for agrarian reform, labor rights, and the phaseout of the U.S. bases.

During this trying period, she also worked out a truce with the Muslim insurgents. More astounding was the historic sixty-day truce she signed with the communist insurgency, bringing peace to the country for the first time in seventeen years.

The peace did not last long. Two events, one on the heels of the other, rocked the country.

On January 22, 10,000 peasants marched to Manila to demand land reform. They had reached Mendiola Bridge near Malacanang Palace when police and marines fired into the line of march, killing eighteen and wounding over one hundred others.

The killings, so reminiscent of the Marcos era, shocked the

At a rally to support the new Philippine constitution, President Aquino sits with Vice-President Salvador Laurel, *above,* and Kris Aquino sings, *below.* NELSON

country. Though an Aquino government investigation brought an immediate apology from the armed forces for their hasty actions, the incident filled many people with foreboding that the government was becoming repressive. A week after this event, police were shunted to side streets while a larger march of peasants, now joined by workers and students, peacefully reached Malacanang, where government officials greeted them.

Alarming as the attack on the first march was, a far more dangerous situation erupted a week later when army rebels staged a military coup and occupied two army bases and a television station. In the wings was Ferdinand Marcos, packed and ready to fly to Manila from Hawaii to declare himself leader of a new government.

The army bases and television station were quickly reclaimed by the loyal army under General Ramos. Marcos was issued orders by the United States government that he may never return to the Philippines unless officially permitted to do so by President Aquino.

The coup failed, but it revealed a critical situation within the armed forces. Clearly, a group of rebels was not loyal to the president and was intent on disrupting the government. More serious was their expressed goal to force President Aquino to adopt conservative policies, especially toward the New People's Army. The rebels, among others, demanded a military campaign against the insurgents.

The inability of President Aquino to deal with the right wing of the army was one reason given by the New People's Army for terminating peace talks. They claimed that President Aquino was giving in to conservative pressure and that she was not sincere in the pursuit of peace. They immediately left Manila for their sanctuaries in the hills to resume, once again, their armed struggle.

These critical events did not diminish President Aquino's popularity. She won endorsement of the new constitution by 75 percent of the voters, a clear signal of continuing Aquino support.

The constitution adopted by the country guarantees civil and human rights. Under it, the president will hold office for a single six-year term, securing President Aquino's tenure until 1992. In some ways the constitution is similar to that of the United States in that it provides for the election of a two-house legislature, for an independent judiciary, and for a system of checks and balances. It also talks of a nuclear-free Philippines, consistent with national interests, and a vote by both the Philippine and the United States senates to determine the renewal or termination of the lease for the two U.S. bases; it bans abortion and empowers the legislature to formulate policies on land reform and welfare programs.

President Aquino knows, as do the millions who have supported her, that she must put the force of her government behind its commitment to basic social reform. By the fall of 1987, eighteen months after she assumed the presidency, her government had failed to propose decisive programs for land reform and economic progress.

In the absence of a strong Aquino voice, the Philippines continue to be rocked by violence, by brutal murders in the countryside, by military skirmishes with the communist insurgents and Moro independence fighters. There are militant working-class strikes, peasant protests, demands for human rights and justice, and a steady call for the phaseout of U.S. bases.

In the unremitting turmoil, the fifth and most dangerous right-wing mutiny came close to overthrowing the Aquino government.

Early August 28, rebel soldiers launched a well-planned strike against Malacanang Palace. They took over an air force and an army base and invaded television stations, over which they broadcast appeals for an uprising to depose the Aquino government.

Not until the next afternoon at 3:00 P.M. did President Aquino address the nation. Encouraged by the immediate announcement of support by the United States government, she urged the civilian population to remain calm while she ordered an all-out military attack on the rebels. She said there would be no compromise with the traitors.

Using aircraft and firing rockets at rebel strongholds, loyal government troops under General Ramos finally subdued the mutiny and placed a thousand soldiers under arrest. In the fighting, more civilians than soldiers were killed. Among the wounded was the president's son, Noynoy.

As crises envelop the Aquino government, the fate of the democratic structure she fought so valiantly to put into place hangs in the balance. The Marcos dictatorship has left her with a military hungry for power and privilege, a military she has not succeeded in placing under civilian control. To appease the rebels, she reluctantly conceded to their demands for higher wages and increased arms. Behind them stand conservative forces determined to put people power into disarray. Unable to come to grips with the problems of unemployment, wage increases, land redistribution, and foreign debt that assail her government, the president is indeed losing the people support that placed her in office.

Whatever changes occur, Corazon C. Aquino has earned a role in history for having been the charismatic force that helped topple the ruthless Marcos dictatorship. In its place she has instituted a democratic form of government. The flow of history will depend on the unity and vitality of the Filipino people to continue their long struggle for human rights and justice, on their insistent demands for progress.

# A Written Interview with President Aquino

During President Aquino's visit to New York in September 1986, her calendar was full. Since I could not get a personal interview, her appointment secretary suggested that I submit a list of questions which President Aquino would try to look at on her return to Manila. I would like to thank the president for finding time in her busy schedule to answer these questions.

Q: In view of your concern for the welfare of children, will your government enact special legislation for their welfare, such as a Federal Children's Bureau?

A: I launched on June 3, 1986, a nationwide drive to promote the well-being and total development of Filipino children and to protect them from exploitation and abuse. An inter-agency task force, which I created to prepare a national plan of action, has been continuously at work. I expect recommendations that will lead to legislation for the welfare of children.

Q:  To help the impoverished until the economy improves, will you be able to enact special social legislation for their care?

A:  Our Congress, whose members will be elected on May 11, will convene in July. I intend to initiate legislation that will provide for the care of children. Its final form will include the recommendations of the task force I had created for the Filipino children.

Q:  Are you also opening the doors of your country to investment by Asian nations such as Japan?

A:  We have opened our doors to investments from Asian countries. In fact, Japan is second only to the United States in total investment in the Philippines. In my visit to ASEAN and Japan last year, I stressed more investments to speed up our economic recovery. Within ASEAN, we have proposed the creation of a Common Market type of cooperation that will lead to closer economic ties.

Q:  Would you today send your children (or grandchildren) to the United States for an education?

A:  I would prefer to have my children study in the Philippines at this time, for no other reason except that we want to stay together as much as possible. However, if my children would express a desire for a U.S. education, I would not object since I was educated there myself.

Q:  You have remarked on the need to talk peace with the insurgents until you have improved the economic conditions that give rise to such a situation. Considering the pressures on you, will you be able to hold out the olive branch, as you put it, until economic conditions improve?

A:  It is obvious that the insurgents would not allow me to hold out the olive branch long enough to make their cause irrelevant. They had broken off the negotiations, and launched attacks on government forces. In my speech at the Philippine Military Academy in Baguio City, on

March 22, 1987, I announced a tougher stand against insurgency.

Q:  Did you try to discourage your husband from returning to the Philippines in 1983?

A:  I tried to but in vain. Although I wished he had stayed with us in Boston, I felt at that time that he belonged more to the Filipino people.

Q:  How do you account for the force and determination of your leadership in view of the passive political role of your past?

A:  As wife of a political leader, I had a close view of political events and the personalities involved. Some writers traced the force and determination of my leadership to my ancestors, one of whom was a member of the Philippine senate and had run for president.

Q:  What would you want U.S. youngsters to know about your country?

A:  I want them to know that the Philippines is a land of friendly and gentle people with their own culture, democratic traditions, and aspirations to live in peace and equality with all nations. I want them to know that aside from being the only Christian nation in Asia—80 percent of our people are Catholics—we were the first to proclaim a Republic in Asia, in 1898, and drafted a constitution in 1899 that can compare with the world's best at that time.

# Suggested Further Reading

Archer, Jules. *The Philippines' Fight for Freedom.* New York: Crowell-Collier Press, 1970.

Bunge, Frederica M., ed. *Philippines, A Country Study.* 3rd ed. Washington: Department of the Army, 1984.

Hill, Gerald N., and Kathleen Thompson Hill, with cooperation of Psinakis, Steve. *The True Story and Analysis of the Aquino Assassination.* Sonoma, California: Hilltop Publishing Company, 1983.

Kerkvliet, Benedict J. *The Huk Rebellion: A Study of Peasant Revolt in the Philippines.* Berkeley: University of California Press, 1982.

Lawson, Don. *The New Philippines.* 2d ed., rev. New York: Franklin Watts, 1986.

Nance, John. *The Land and People of the Philippines.* Philadelphia: J. B. Lippincott Company, 1977.

Schirmer, Daniel B., and Stephen Rosskamm Shalom, eds. *The Philippines Reader.* Boston: South End Press, 1987.

Zich, Arthur. "Hope and Danger in the Philippines," *National Geographic,* July 1986, pp. 76–118.

# Index

Page numbers in *italics* refer to captions.

2